THE CASINO SWITCHEROO

THE TRAVELERS BOOK SEVEN

MICHAEL P. KING

Blurred Lines Press

The Casino Switcheroo

Michael P. King

ISBN 978-0-9993648-7-1

Cover design by Paramita Bhattacharjee at creativeparamita.com

The Casino Switcheroo is a work of fiction. The names, characters, places, and events are products of the author's imagination or are used fictitiously. Any similarity to real persons or places is entirely coincidental.

"Another full-throttle installment that shows that this crime series has no intention of slowing down."—*Kirkus Reviews*

Trust him at your peril...

When Koenig, the Traveling Man's original mentor, shows up touting a casino heist—a once-in-a-lifetime, high-stakes robbery—all the Traveling Man can think about is stealing the score.

His wife thinks he's crazy.

Koenig is a puppet master—a master manipulator who compartmentalizes the parts of a job so that only he knows all the details. What are they really going to steal? Who's going to carry it out? How are they going to escape? And who's going to be discarded to the opposition or the law?

The Travelers will have their hands full staying alive and staying free, and outthinking the other players, if they hope to steal Koenig's loot right from under his nose.

The Casino Switcheroo is a no-holds-barred page turner. If you like can't-figure-them-out plot twists, fast-paced action, and criminal mischief, you'll love the seventh book in the Travelers series.

For Sarah, my only one

1

THE OLD MAN

The Traveling Man, a con man going by the name Paul Longmont, parked his Cadillac Escalade about twenty feet away from the blue BMW facing Lake Dunville, a small lake on a county park outside Madisonville. Paul was six feet, medium build, his gray-streaked hair cut short around the sides. He had a face that was hard to remember and a manner that said he knew what he was talking about. He took a Smith &Wesson .38 out of his suit coat pocket and lay it in the passenger's seat before he got out of his SUV. The clouds were darkening, and the waves were pitching up angry on the water. On the far side of the lake, a fishing boat was trolling back to the dock. Paul hoped to be back in his Cadillac before the storm broke. As he crossed the deserted parking lot to the BMW, a bodyguard, a big man in a dark suit who moved like a professional soldier, got out of the front seat passenger's side and gestured for Paul to stop. Paul raised his arms. The bodyguard frisked him and then opened the back seat door. Paul climbed in.

His wife, going by the name Jessie Taggert, was sitting on the other side of the mark, Hugo Lansing. She was effortlessly beautiful. Tight clothes, athletic build, long dark hair—guessing her age would be an exercise in miscalculation. Paul hadn't seen her in the two months she'd been worming her way into Lansing's life. God, he'd missed her. She gave him the neutral look reserved for someone she'd never seen before.

Lansing, the stock image of a CEO with his perfect haircut and his tailored suit, flashed a smile. "How's your day so far?"

"No complaints," Paul replied.

"I understand we have a mutual friend?"

"Vicki Brassos."

"She still out in the Caymans?"

"Lawyers sorted that out. Last month she was in LA. I don't know where she is today, so if she still owes you money, you're out of luck."

"Who said she owed me money?"

"Come on, she owes everybody money."

"You, too, huh?"

Paul shrugged. "Not to be rude, but are you ready to get down to business?"

Lansing nodded. "I'm listening."

"We going to have this conversation with her sitting in here?"

Jessie put her hand on the door handle. "I can wait outside with Tony."

Lansing patted her knee. "It's not a problem."

"It's your party," Paul replied. "Can you get me the bearer bonds?"

"Five hundred thousand in untraceable bonds. That's going to cost you six hundred thousand."

"One hundred thousand for the service? That's kind of steep."

"That's the way it is. With all the new banking regulations, moving cash around is expensive. And bearer bonds are harder and harder to find."

"How about five hundred fifty?"

"Six hundred thousand. Look around. If you can do better, you won't hurt my feelings."

"Okay," Paul said. "I guess I'll have to eat it. How do you want to go about this?"

"I've got a place I like to meet in an office park. You bring the cash;

I'll have the bonds. We'll run the money through a counter while you verify the bonds, then we all go our merry ways."

"How do I know you won't try to jack me?"

"You know who I am. You think that's how I make a living?"

"How soon can you get the bonds?"

"How soon can you get the money?"

"The day after tomorrow."

"I'll call with the details on the day of."

Paul got out of the BMW. Rain was starting to fall, fat drops bouncing off the pavement. He jogged back to his Cadillac. Everything was going to plan. Jessie was doing her job to perfection. She was obviously the trusted girlfriend. He started his SUV, turned on the wipers, and waited for the BMW to leave.

TONY GOT BACK into the front seat passenger's side. Lansing tapped the back of the driver's seat. "Let's go, Sam." The BMW drove out of the parking lot and back through the woods to the county highway.

"So what do you think?" Lansing asked.

"I don't trust that guy," Jessie said.

"Of course not. He's a criminal. But he's not going to screw me."

"How can you be so sure?"

"Self-interest. He needs to get rid of a pile of cash, make it portable, get to a place where he can safely store it. He can't do that himself. So he's got to play straight with me."

"But where do the bonds come from?"

"I've got another client who wants to get rid of them. He needs the cash. So I get paid for doing the exchange. That's how I make a living. Adding value."

She leaned against him and rested her hand on his thigh. "I don't know how you do it."

He kissed her. "I've been at this a long time."

Thunder boomed in the distance, and rain pounded the roof of the car.

. . .

MEANWHILE, halfway across the country, Alexander Koenig, an old, bald man with a bushy white mustache, dressed in a seersucker suit, sat at a green picnic table at a freeway rest stop next to Raymond, his lieutenant, a tall, skinny man with slicked-back blond hair. Across from them sat Carlos Hernandez, a barrel-chested Latino wearing expensive casual clothes.

Hernandez took a toothpick out of his mouth. "So you want eleven guys—eight plus three."

"Including you," Koenig said. "You'll lead seven. Raymond will lead three."

Hernandez continued. "All shooters, one demolition expert?"

"That's right. And I'm talking about serious men—the kind of men who don't blink or run."

"For how long?"

"Three weeks. We'll make sure everyone is comfortable with everyone else, finalize the details, and then we'll do the job."

"How much money?"

"For the guys? Ten thousand apiece. For you, twice that."

"I can get all the men you want for ten thousand each, but my cut needs to be twenty-five thousand."

Koenig smiled. "For you, Carlos, I won't even argue. Twenty-five thousand it is."

Koenig and Hernandez shook hands over the table. Then Raymond handed Koenig a cell phone. Koenig passed it to Hernandez. "There's one number in the speed dial. We meet in Bathsheba City in a week. You get your people together, make a call, and Raymond will arrange transportation and lodging."

"So who are we killing, and what are we blowing up?" Hernandez asked.

"You know how I work. You'll know when it's time. That's why the cops are never on one of my jobs."

Hernandez pushed himself up from the picnic table. Koenig and Raymond watched him cross the parking lot to a Ford F-150 pickup truck. "You think he's reliable?" Raymond asked.

"Completely reliable. I've used him four times. He's never let me down. And if he lives, he'll be worth every penny."

"I heard from Lulu and JB. Between the two of them, they have the run of the casino-hotel. JB was babbling about a codebook that was going to be in a room safe. I guessed it was something you told him," Raymond said.

"An extra incentive to focus his attention."

"So we're all set?"

"For the job, yes. For the sleight of hand, no. Have you been keeping track of that couple I told you to watch?" Koenig asked.

"Yeah. They've got a scam going on with the money launderer Lansing. It's tough staying off their radar."

"Just keep an eye out for when they pull the trigger. Then we'll see if we can rope them into our scheme."

THE NEXT DAY, Jessie, wrapped in a towel, stood out on the swimming pool patio behind Lansing's mansion, a Greek Revival in the old-money part of town. She had a cigarette in one hand and her phone in the other.

"Is everything as advertised?" Paul asked.

"Yeah. Hold on." She walked to the far side of the pool. "It took long enough, but I finally got all the way in. Acting so clueless all the time was getting tedious."

"Any suspicions about your cover? Any questions at all?"

"No, I'm just a three-time divorcee with few scruples and a taste for excitement. My second husband—what a whiny little bitch. We're lucky Lansing prefers age-appropriate women."

"Baby, you're every middle-aged man's wet dream. He couldn't possibly resist you. It just takes time. Now we're finally there. Only one more day."

"He's going to pick up the bonds tomorrow morning, then call you, so our window is tight."

"I'll press to meet in the late afternoon. That will give you the time to work your magic."

. . .

THAT EVENING, Lansing sat at the cherrywood desk in his home office, talking on his smartphone. The room had been staged by an interior designer to impress visitors. A bookcase of unread books stood against the inside wall, tasteful impressionistic paintings hung on the other walls, and the window curtains assured privacy while framing a view of the back patio and swimming pool. "That's right, Saul, this is the best opportunity you're going to have to get rid of the bonds."

"But four hundred and fifty thousand dollars?"

"I know that seems low, but no one will give you face value. If someone would, you'd have traded them already. That's just the way it is."

The line was quiet for a moment. "Okay, if it's the best you can do," Saul said.

"It is. I'll be by to pick them up at nine a.m." He ended the call. He'd make $150,000 tomorrow. Easy money. Unless Paul Longmont planned to cheat him.

Sam, loose suit and the bent nose of an ex-boxer, came into the office. "I ran that trace for you."

"What did you find?"

"That phone Jessie's been calling? It moves around town, but it spends a lot of time at an apartment on South Elm."

"South Elm? Send Tony around there to have a look."

"You got it." Sam shifted his weight from one foot to the other, his hands clasped behind his back.

"What?"

"If you don't trust her, maybe she shouldn't be living in the house."

"I trust her. I just—I'm just worried, okay?"

"Then why don't you just ask her who she's calling?"

"Check out that apartment."

TONY CLIMBED out of an old Ford Bronco and walked across the street to the Crest View Apartments on South Elm Street. He was dressed casually—jeans, gym shoes. A black windbreaker covered the pistol he wore in a shoulder rig. The apartment building had seen better days. The front door was scratched and dented, and the lock was broken. He stepped into the entry and read off the names on the mailboxes. Nothing stood out. Three apartments on each floor. Three floors. He walked down the hallway, listening at each door. TV, family noises, just what you would expect after supper in a normal apartment. He walked up to the second floor. Only one resident seemed to be home. Then he walked up to the third floor. Two home for sure. He went back downstairs and out to the Bronco. Three residents still out. Second-shift worker? Somebody gone out to the movies? Jessie's sick old mom? Didn't have to be her secret lover. He lowered the Bronco's window. Mr. Lansing would expect him to wait awhile, so that's what he was going to do.

PAUL WAS PARKED down the street in a Corolla he'd stolen that morning. He'd gone out to dinner and had come back just in time to see Tony go into the building. Luck was a great gift. And he was always lucky when it came to closing a deal. But why was Tony here? Jessie had never been near this place. And there was nothing to connect Jessie with him. The only time they'd been together in the last two months was yesterday in Lansing's car. He let his mind roll through the variables. The phone. Jessie had done her job too well. Lansing must be jealous. Must have someone tracking her calls. But Paul needed to be sure. He texted her. *Your data plan is at five percent.* Immediately, she texted back, *OK.* So she was safe. No need to abort. Everything was ready. As soon as Tony left, he'd get his gear out of the apartment and go to a motel for the night.

THE NEXT DAY at three o'clock in the afternoon, Paul sat at the window of a third-floor apartment looking through the scope of his sniper rifle at Lansing's mansion across the street. Jessie was certainly taking her time. Afternoon delight. She was thorough, that's for sure. But there was nothing to worry about. She had Lansing wrapped around her finger. Paul scanned the front of the mansion. Still, he wished she'd hurry up. The longer she took, the more opportunity there was for something to go wrong.

JESSIE, her dark hair cascading down her back, tiptoed out the dim bedroom with her clothes bundled under one arm and a briefcase in her other hand. Lansing snored softly from his side of the king-size bed. She smiled. He was a good-looking guy, not too selfish in bed, and he fell asleep afterward as if on cue. If only they were all like that. On the landing at the top of the stairs, she set the briefcase on a side table and put on her panties and bra. She glanced over her shoulder at the bedroom door and then down the stairs. Silence. She pulled her dress on over her head, picked up her high heels and the briefcase and crept quietly down the stairs. Where were Tony and Sam?

On the front porch of the mansion, she leaned against a pillar to slip on her shoes. The cars weren't in the driveway, and there was no one in sight. Her phone buzzed in her pocket. She answered it as she started down the brick walkway. "Hey, honey."

"All done?" Paul asked.

"I've got the bearer bonds."

"Good girl."

"I don't know. It was just too easy."

"Sometimes they are."

"Not like this."

"But you're sure the bonds are real?"

"Absolutely. I watched him check them over before he put them in the case."

"And he's not on to you?"

"Please."

"Then what are you worried about?"

She came through the gate in the wrought-iron fence at the bottom of the driveway. "Where are the bodyguards? Have they both gone for a piss? And where are the cars? They usually leave them out during the day." She glanced down the street. "Where are you?"

"I'm up in an apartment across the street. I'm watching you through my rifle scope. There's a red Audi parked at the corner. Keys behind the driver's side front wheel."

"Thanks, baby."

"You bet."

PAUL STOOD at the window and watched her drive away. The mansion was quiet. No one was following her. She'd done exceptional work. All they had to do now was sell the bonds back to Lansing, ten cents on the dollar. Not as much money as they might have hoped for, but no muss, no fuss. They'd be out of town before tomorrow and on vacation for the next few months.

He lowered the window and turned back into the apartment. Time to get out of here. The Everets always got home from work shortly after 5:00 p.m. The sniper rifle case lay open on the dining room table. He disassembled the rifle into the case, pressing each part into its foam cutout. As he closed the lid, he felt his smartphone vibrate. Text message. *He's on to you. He knows where you're staying. He's sending a team.* Paul slipped his phone back into his pants pocket. Jessie was right. No problem. Plenty of time to get ready.

An hour later, up in a high-rise condo overlooking the city, Paul and Jessie weren't lying in bed drinking margaritas and toasting their success, or standing on the balcony watching the traffic far below, or even making the phone call to set up the money swap. No, they were sitting at the dining room table, watching the screen on a laptop computer. Paul had his smartphone in his hand.

On the computer, they heard the door being kicked in and saw four men rush into the apartment on South Elm, guns blazing. Paul input 911. He put on a panicked voice. "Help. Home invasion. 3417 South Elm, apartment nine. We're hiding in the bedroom closet." He ended the call.

They watched the men moving through the apartment, spraying bullets into the rooms before they entered.

Jessie patted his hand. "What's the response time to that apartment?"

"First response should be four minutes. It's a shame we can't stay and watch."

"I know I usually bitch about the three-way split with the inside man, but this time he's earning every penny."

"We'll never know what tipped Lansing, or why he let you walk away," Paul said.

"Wanted to catch you."

"Maybe he couldn't quite believe that you'd do it."

"Dreamer."

Paul closed the laptop. "I've missed you so much."

"I'm back now." She kissed him. "Time to go."

She grabbed up the briefcase containing the bearer bonds. They walked down the hall to the fire exit. Paul eased the fire door open and pointed his Glock down the stairwell. No ambush team was waiting for them. "Come on."

At the bottom of the stairs, he pushed through the emergency exit. Their black Ford Explorer was still parked on the street. No one was challenging them. No one was shooting at them. "Four guys. Sent to the wrong address. I'm beginning to feel a little insulted."

"Count your blessings."

They climbed into the Explorer. Jessie got out her phone. "The clock is running. Lansing will be expecting a phone call from his guys in the next few minutes."

Paul pulled away from the curb. "Then let's not disappoint."

She made the call. "Sugar?"

"What?" Lansing asked.

"We've still got the bonds. Your guys made a hell of a mess, if that's any consolation."

"What do you want?"

"Fifty thousand dollars, cash."

"No way."

"That's ten cents on the dollar. Very generous and very doable. You need these bonds, and you've got that much cash in your safe."

"I'm going to kill you and whoever you're working with."

"Maybe. But in the meantime, you're going to meet us in thirty minutes at a location I'm going to text to you. You're going to bring the cash, and you're going to buy back these bonds. Unless you want to go to your client meeting with your dick in your hand. Of course, that might be interesting to watch. And honey pie, that's just you, Tony, and the money. Anyone more, and I burn the bonds. See you soon."

She turned to Paul. "We still going to the school?"

"Yeah, that one glitch doesn't change anything, particularly with the tight timeline."

They drove across town to the abandoned campus of Bright Futures Industrial College, a bankrupt for-profit university. Weeds were growing through the cracks in the parking lot. The walls were painted with elaborate graffiti and some of the windows were boarded up. The area back by the picnic tables was littered with fast-food trash and shattered beer bottles. They backed up to the garage door of the automotive repair department.

"You check the back, and I'll check the front," Paul said.

"I thought I was doing the swap."

"That was before the glitch. I'd rather have you up high now. You're a better shot than me, anyway."

She rolled her eyes. "You aren't even trying to sell that."

"I'm not changing my mind. The sniper rifle is in the back."

She picked the lock on the garage door, raised it, and carried the sniper rifle back though the gloom to the stolen Ford Focus that was parked at the garage door on the other side. The automotive repair department was empty except for some built-in tool tables, but it still smelled of oil and industrial cleanser. The Focus was just as they had left it. Shotguns laying in the front seat and their roller bags in the trunk. She left the trunk open. Then she climbed the stairs to the second-floor catwalk that ran the perimeter of the garage. At the front of the building, she set up the sniper rifle to cover the parking lot beyond the Explorer. She checked the magazine—it was full—and inserted it into the rifle before she got out her phone. "Honey, we're good to go."

"Text him."

The sun was low, casting long shadows across the parking lot, when the blue BMW pulled into the lot and wound its way back to the automotive repair department. When it stopped, Paul got out of the Explorer wearing a Kevlar vest. A black ski mask covered his face, an assault rifle was slung over his right shoulder, his finger beside the trigger, and he had the briefcase in his left hand. Two men got out of the BMW, Lansing and Tony. Lansing carried a satchel. Tony wore a Kevlar vest over his shirt and tie. A pistol was holstered at his hip.

"The bonds in there?" Lansing asked.

"Your boy stays where he is. He holds his hands at head height. You come forward to the bumper of the Explorer. He moves, I kill you first."

Tony raised his hands. Lansing started forward, then stopped. His mouth fell open. "My God. It's you. You're Paul Longmont. Buying the bonds was just a scam so you could steal them."

Paul dropped the briefcase and held the assault rifle in both hands. "Keep moving. Keep moving if you want to live."

Lansing walked up to front bumper of the Explorer.

"Put the satchel on the hood and open it."

"Show me the bonds."

"First things first. The bonds are worthless to me—too hard to cash. You're the only one who wants them. Put the satchel on the hood."

Lansing opened the satchel. Paul saw bundles of one hundred-dollar bills.

"Step back."

Lansing stepped back from the Explorer. Paul tossed the briefcase to him. Lansing caught it in both arms. Paul raked his left hand through the money in the satchel. It was all there. Lansing opened the case and thumbed through the bonds. "I'm going to kill you. I'm going to kill you both."

"Another day," Paul said. He picked up the satchel and started backing toward the garage door. Tony reached for his gun. Jessie put a round in the asphalt at his feet. He stopped reaching. Paul pulled down the garage door. Jessie put another round in the asphalt and watched as Lansing and Tony got back into their BMW and drove back through the parking lot. Then she scrambled down the stairs with the rifle to meet Paul at the Ford Focus. She tossed the rifle into the trunk and slammed it shut while Paul raised the garage door. They rolled out into an alley and turned left onto a side street behind the college.

In town traffic was light. In a few minutes they were on the freeway headed north. No one was tailing them. Paul pulled off at the first rest stop. Three semitrucks were parked in the rest lane and five cars were parked in front of the information center. A red Subaru Forester was parked next to the dog-walking area at the far end of the parking lot. They pulled in beside it. A skinny Latino dressed in gym clothes got out of the Subaru and climbed into the back seat of the Ford Focus.

"Roberto," Paul said, "thanks for the heads up."

"Hey, man, I wasn't getting paid if I let him kill you."

Jessie smiled. "Fifty thousand. Five thousand for expenses leaves forty-five thousand, divided by three makes your end fifteen thousand." She counted out the money into a grocery bag and passed it back to him. "Count it."

He thumbed through the money, smiled and nodded. "A pleasure doing business with you."

Paul studied him carefully. "I don't have to tell you what will happen if he finds out you screwed him."

"He's not finding out. I'm going to trickle this money out."

"Good luck."

Roberto climbed out of the car. Paul and Jessie watched him drive away. Then Paul pulled off his tactical gear and tossed it into the back seat, while Jessie put the $35,000 in a shopping bag. They took their roller bags from the trunk and crossed the parking lot to the information center. A mom with two grade schoolers was standing in front of the vending machines.

"Need anything?" Paul asked.

Jessie shook her head. She stuffed the empty satchel into a trash can. They rolled their bags out into the parking lot on the other side of the information center. Their gray Cadillac was parked on the far side of the lot away from the building. Paul pressed his key fob. The trunk opened. He took out his phone. "Billy? Got a pickup for you. Blue Ford Focus full of prime gear. Rest stop just north of Madisonville."

"I'll put the trade-in value on your tab."

"Thanks."

He put his phone away. They loaded their roller bags and the shopping bag into the trunk. Just as he shut the lid, he heard a voice calling to him.

He turned. An old, bald man with a bushy white mustache, wearing a wrinkled seersucker suit, was walking toward them. He spoke in a soft voice. "Hey, kid."

Paul shook his head slowly. "Koenig. Why aren't you dead?"

"That's what I've always liked about you, straight to the point. Not surprised to see me. No how you doing."

"We were just leaving."

"Who is this guy?" Jessie asked.

"He never told you about me?" Koenig asked. "I raised him from a pup. Fed him from my hand until he was old enough to earn his way."

"What do you want?" Paul asked.

"That was a nice little job you pulled. Not very many moving parts. Only one wrench in the works. The shot-up apartment was a little much, but you were never afraid to make change- ups on the fly."

"How long you been dogging us?"

"Long enough to see if you still had the juice."

"So I guess this means you're convinced."

"I'm putting a job together."

"We're going on vacation."

"This is a high-dollar, once-in-a-lifetime score. I need the best." He held his jacket open and turned in a circle. "I'm on the up-and-up.

Let's eat some supper. My treat. You don't like what you hear, you walk away. But I'm telling you, you're going to like what you hear."

Paul gestured toward a white Toyota Highlander. "That yours?"

Koenig nodded.

"We'll follow you. If we're still behind you when you get to the restaurant, we'll come in."

They followed the Highlander out of the rest stop. It was dark now, and rush hour was long over, but plenty of aggressive drivers were still jockeying through the lanes. "Anyone following us?"

Jessie turned in her seat. "No," she said. "But I didn't know that guy had been watching us the last few days."

"I know."

She looked down the highway toward the Highlander for a moment, and then turned to Paul. "You don't like that guy."

"It's not about like or don't like. You've never met a manipulator like him. He's like the snake in the Garden of Eden. It doesn't matter what he says or how much he helps you, he's got no principles. It's always part of a complex plan that benefits only him."

"Did he really bring you up? Take you under his wing, like you did for me?"

"Not like I did for you."

"But he was your mentor?"

"Remember I told you my folks were messed up? That they landed in jail, and I ran away from the foster home?"

"Yeah."

"He found me mopping up in a bar. He became my 'dad,' used me until I figured him out. By then I knew enough to find crews on my own. Flash forward to that sunny day when I spotted you. We shouldn't even be going to this meeting."

"Then why are we?"

"I don't know. Maybe I just want to see if I can resist him, see through his game, screw him over."

"Who told me dick-measuring contests were one of the quickest ways to end up screwed?"

"I know. Maybe I should have just shot him in the parking lot."

They followed the Highlander into the gravel parking lot of the Holiday Barbeque. The flashing neon sign attached to the roof had two dead spots that made it flash *Ho day beque*. There were more than a dozen cars in the lot, but there were several empty spots at the front of the building. Inside, the restaurant smelled of hickory smoke and stale beer. Country top forty blasted from the sound system. The hostess sat them at a four top in the back corner: Paul, Jessie, Koenig, and a tall man with slicked-back blond hair. Their waitress—a skinny, middle-aged woman wearing dangling earrings and a black apron over her T-shirt and jeans—brought water and menus.

"Who's this guy?" Paul asked.

"He's Raymond," Koenig said. "He drives for me."

"And what's your name?" Raymond asked.

Paul smiled. "Your boss didn't tell you? We don't have names."

"That's kind of inconvenient, isn't it?"

"For who?" Paul turned to Koenig. "So how did you find us?"

"I've still got a few tricks up my sleeve. Let's just say we use a number of the same vendors."

Paul scanned the room, studying the other diners, the movement of the servers, the feel of the Holiday Barbeque experience. This place was certainly noisy enough for a private conversation. And the other diners—couples and threesomes mainly—were certainly chomping away with gusto, but there was something about this restaurant that just wasn't normal.

Their waitress returned. She pulled a pad from her apron. "What'll it be?"

Koenig started. "I'll have the small rib plate, no sides, and a tap beer."

"Give me the barbeque sandwich combo," Raymond said.

Jessie smiled. "Nothing for me."

The waitress turned to Paul.

"Just coffee."

The waitress left the table. Paul took another look around and then tapped his hand on the table. "Now I get it. This place is mobbed up."

Koenig shrugged.

"You pay protection?"

"Friends of friends."

"So why have you gone to all this trouble to find me?"

"I'm getting too old for the game. Don't laugh. It's true. I've put one last job together to fill out my retirement money. This is a once-in-a-lifetime, totally impossible sleight of hand. People in the know will be talking about this for years to come."

"I'm listening."

"I've got all my players in place. But two of my inside people— clean for years—relapsed. Can't wait for them to clean up. Hell, I don't know if I could trust them now, anyway. So I need a couple of top-notch operators. That's where you come in. I could have made do with my other people, but you know me, I like all the positions filled. So I figured why not ask the kid? All he can do is say no. He's no fool. He'll know a sweet job when he sees it."

"So what's the job?"

"You'll work undercover about a month. You'll prep the field of play with another couple—you know, scout the layout, collect door and safe codes, figure out the timelines. No risk at all for you, and you take home one hundred thousand. Bet you can't say you made near that much on that little run-and-gun you just got out of. You say you're in, I'll tell you the details."

The waitress brought their drinks.

Paul looked from Koenig to Raymond and back. He felt a queasy fluttering in his belly—like he was about to do something he'd regret for a long time. "Tomorrow. I'll let you know something tomorrow."

"Excellent. There's a Perkins on Seventh Street. We'll meet for breakfast at eight o'clock."

"If we're in, we'll be there," Paul said. He turned to Jessie. "Let's go."

They drove back into Madisonville to the first interchange, went through a Taco Delight drive-through to get some dinner, and checked into a Budget Inn. The parking in front of their room was full, so they ended up parked under the Budget Inn sign. They rolled their bags across the parking lot to their room.

Once inside, Jessie lifted her bag onto the bed nearest the door. "We shouldn't even be in this state. Lansing will be gunning for us. Besides, you already said that the old man can't be trusted. The money is just too good for the work he sketched out."

Paul shut the motel room door. "You're right on both counts. I should have said no, but I didn't."

He left his bag by the door and sat down on the bed closest to the bathroom. She sat down beside him. "What's up with you?"

"This is going to sound crazy. But you know that thing where you find yourself falling back into an old relationship that isn't you anymore? You go back to your old neighborhood, and instead of being the person you are now, you're the runt who's always being picked on. Or you go to see your mom, and she asks you to do something, and you don't want to do it, and you can't tell her it's bullshit. You know what I'm talking about?"

"Yes, I do." She squeezed his hand. "So we should get back in the car and get the hell out of here. Drive like crazy for two or three days. Make sure he can't find us. Spend a couple of days in a honeymoon suite."

"That would be the smart play."

"But that's not what you want to do. Are you insane? You just told me that you're vulnerable to being played by this guy, and you've told me he's the devil."

"Not the devil."

"The fucking snake in the fucking Garden of Eden. Satan. The devil." She sprang up and started pacing back and forth between the door and the bed. "Jesus. You're going to be the death of us yet."

"I've always dreamed of beating him at his own game."

"Let me rewind the tape so that you can listen to yourself. This is exactly how we end up screwed. He saw you coming. That's why he wants you in. He knows he can play you—that your history together is going to fuck with your mind."

"Yep. But I'm not by myself. I'm with you. He doesn't know

anything about you. He doesn't think you're my partner; he thinks you're my tasty bit. My honey trap. That's where he's going to make his mistake."

"So we're going to get inside his game and steal his score—his retirement plan, his score of a lifetime?"

"That's our plan."

"He's going to be expecting it."

"That's what makes it so sweet. Our timing has to be perfect. And we aren't the only ones who are going to be trying to screw him. Everybody working this score will be planning to take the money as soon as it's in hand."

She sat back down beside him. "We bail when I say bail. Doesn't matter how close we are to having it all. Staying alive and staying free are more important than any score."

"Absolutely."

"Take my hand and look me in the eye. Say it."

He gripped her hand. He didn't blink. "We bail when you say bail."

THE NEXT MORNING, Koenig and Raymond were already seated in a booth at the Perkins when Paul and Jessie pushed through the glass doors. The restaurant was still busy with the tail end of the morning rush, waitresses carrying trays loaded with pancakes and omelets, customers slurping coffee and chattering in that highly caffeinated morning way. They slid into the booth, Paul next to Koenig, Jessie next to Raymond.

Koenig smiled. "So you're in?"

"We're in."

"Have you eaten?"

Paul shook his head. Koenig pushed a menu toward him and motioned to a waitress. They all ordered food and coffee. After she left the booth, Paul gave Koenig a significant look. "Fill in the details."

"Have you heard of Solomon Island?" Koenig asked.

"The casino off the coast of Bathsheba City? You won't be able to break into the vault."

"Won't need to. The casino robbery is our diversion."

"I'm listening."

"The casino is the money laundry for the Smithson crew. Every month money arrives to be cleaned—over one million dollars. It comes in by boat at the VIP marina. That's the score."

"You're crazy. There'll be goons all over that cash. It'd be a bloodbath."

"Usually I'd agree. But next month is old man Smithson's birthday. He's having his party on the island. The big seven zero. All his family and top lieutenants will be there. So during the party, we pull the fake casino robbery. While that's ongoing, we rob all their room safes. Jewelry and cash. That should be one hundred grand easy. And during all the hullabaloo, we take the cash at the marina. By the time they figure out what we're really up to—what with protecting the family and dealing with the robbery—we'll be long gone."

"I can see it," Paul said. "And if robbing the room safes doesn't work out; no harm, no foul."

Koenig nodded. "We've got two players on the inside already. You and your girl will work with them. There're no guns allowed on the island. Everyone comes through metal detectors in a kill box when they come off the ferry from the mainland. You all will time off the security teams, scout the best place to land the heavy gear, gain control of a room key master pass card and the room safe master password, find out the exact time of the festivities and the money delivery."

"Why don't you just bribe an employee?"

"How do you think I found out what I already know? But no one with precise information of the details can be trusted to not sell us out to Smithson."

"So we set up the whole scam for you, provide all the intel, for one hundred thousand?"

"You've got help."

"It's not enough money."

"I don't want to argue about it. You can keep everything in the safes over eighty grand."

"Sixty."

Koenig shrugged. "Okay."

The waitress brought their food. "Anything else?" she asked.

"It's all good," Raymond replied.

Koenig continued. "Time is of the essence."

"We can be in Bathsheba City tomorrow. Fill us in on our covers, and we'll be on our way."

"You're replacement employees, married, front desk and maintenance department." He set a smartphone down next to Paul's plate. "Everything you need to know is on here."

"What're our names?"

"Max and Kelly Jo Barlow."

"We'll have to get IDs."

Koenig pushed an envelope across the table. "Drivers' licenses and Social."

"You were mighty sure of yourself."

He shrugged. "It was worth taking the chance."

Paul reached for the maple syrup. "We better fuel up for the road."

A HALF HOUR LATER, Max and Kelly Jo were crossing the Perkins parking lot. "You want to drive first?" he asked.

"Sure."

He handed her the car fob.

She pressed the button to unlock the doors on the Cadillac. "That guy creeps me out."

"Who? Koenig or Raymond?" Max asked.

"Koenig. Raymond is just muscle."

"He acts like muscle, but he's got to be Koenig's protégé, or he wouldn't have been at the table."

"I still don't think he's got much going on."

Kelly Jo put the Cadillac in gear and backed out of the parking spot. Max turned on the smartphone Koenig had given him and started looking through the screens. They were four blocks from the interstate and twenty hours—more or less—from Bathsheba City. "Do you believe the numbers?" Kelly Jo asked.

"A million dollars? It's bullshit. I don't even believe the job. We'll have to figure it out on the fly. How much of Koenig's story holds up? We know the job's on the island. And we know it's not the casino vault. So what is it? Is it a money delivery? Or is the job something else? If it is the dirty money, does the cash come in by boat? Maybe it comes in via a supply truck. We have to know what the job is so we can be at the right place at the right time. And you can forget about our payment. No matter what we're really stealing, at some point in this job he's going to try to screw us out of our end. That's the way he works."

"And you still don't think that maybe we're in over our heads?"

"Like I said before, everyone involved in this job is going to try to screw everyone else. That's what gives us our edge. We just have to figure out what's really going on in time to set our own play. We've got most of a month. We can use Lansing's money to set ourselves up."

"We're going to need a partner."

"A partner who can deal with weapons and transport."

Kelly Jo took a right turn onto the freeway entrance ramp. A semi-truck blew past just before she merged. "What do you think of my new name?"

"Kelly Jo? I wouldn't have picked it, but it rolls off the tongue well enough."

"I don't like the name Max."

"Well, it's my name now, so you better get used to saying it. Besides, we can save the new IDs we were planning to use after the Lansing job."

"Put them in a Mail-N-More PO box when we get to Bathsheba City?"

"You're reading my mind."

.   .   .

MEANWHILE, Koenig and Raymond sat at the booth in the Perkins surrounded by dirty breakfast dishes. Koenig has a satisfied smile on his face.

Raymond shook his head. "Do you think he believes you?"

"Doesn't matter if he believes me, so long as he does his part."

"I still don't know why we need them. I know he's an expert and all that, but I could run the inside."

"Because they're going to be part of our patsy team. They'll be the only ones with their fingerprints on this job. And we're going to leave them behind."

"You must really hate this guy."

"If I wanted him dead, I'd kill him. I've chosen him because I think he'll wriggle out of the trap. Smithson will waste valuable time looking for him when he should be looking for us. By the time he figures out what really happened, if he ever does, we'll be long gone. That's the kind of failsafe that's priceless."

LATER THAT DAY in Bathsheba City, in the offices of Galaxy Yacht Sales at the city marina, Jeffery Smithson sat behind his mahogany partners desk in his private office. His skin was like crinkled tissue paper, and his thin, gray hair was slathered across his scalp. His two lieutenants sat in chairs facing him. Harold O'Brian, who ran the Solomon Island Casino Resort and oversaw illegal gambling and the money laundry, was a small, soft man with a tiny mustache who wore a banker's pinstripe suit. David Ninovich, who ran the drug operation and a car theft ring from a series of car and truck repair garages, was a beefy, bald man with thick forearms who wouldn't have looked out of place in a mechanic's shop. Smithson started coughing. The aide standing behind him, a bodybuilder in an ill-fitting suit, shook a rescue inhaler and handed it to him. Smithson used the inhaler, tossed it onto the desk, and gave O'Brian a questioning glance.

"Offices were swept this morning, sir."

"Good. Let me get right to it. I'm going to step down after my birthday."

"What?" Ninovich asked. "That's next month. How long have you been thinking about this?"

"Doctors say I don't have any choice."

"What does Tim think?" O'Brian asked.

"He thinks I should have stepped down back when his mother was still alive. Maybe he's right. But enough about that. This is how we're going to move forward. Each of you will keep the businesses you run. And David, you'll keep moving all your money through the casino. Harold will get ten percent for cleaning the cash."

"Okay," Ninovich said.

"And both of you will kick back two percent into my bank safe deposit box. That's your tax."

O'Brian and Ninovich nodded.

"Okay then. Right after my birthday we switch to the new system." Smithson waved them away.

Ninovich followed O'Brian as they left Smithson's office. Twelve percent. That's what Smithson's retirement was going to cost him. Eighty-eight percent was better than his current cut, but still. He had the largest crew and made the most money. That was just the nature of the drug game and the car theft game. Why should he have to pay O'Brian? Why shouldn't he just be the boss? As long as Smithson still got his two percent, why should he care?

Ninovich pushed his way through the front door. The problem was that he didn't know anything about the money laundry and the gambling, and he wasn't networked with all the bureaucrats who had to be paid off. So he couldn't rush things. The first step would be to convince O'Brian that his life would be unchanged if he let him be the boss. Then he could take his time learning the gambling and the money laundry.

Out in the parking lot, O'Brian was waiting for him. "I certainly wasn't expecting that."

"Me, neither," Ninovich replied. "But is was bound to happen sometime."

"So it's congratulations all around."

"Yeah, we're bosses next month."

"And it's a fair deal."

"I'm not bitching about the ten percent, if that's what you're worried about."

"I'm glad to hear it. We don't need trouble. Trouble is expensive."

"That's for sure. And processing the cash is a headache, so I'm happy you've got to do it."

O'Brian smiled. "See you around."

Ninovich watched O'Brian walk away. It really wouldn't take that long. He'd sideline O'Brian, take over his businesses, and push him out. It would be a mistake to break up Smithson's organization.

A week later, Kelly Jo stood behind the hotel reception counter of the Solomon Island Casino Resort. She wore a blue receptionist's skirt suit with the top button of her blouse unbuttoned to expose a hint of her lacy bra. No one was in line to check in, so she'd been passing the time by flirting with a potbellied gambler who'd just arrived for the weekend. Lulu, the female half of the other team Koenig had in place, was also working as a receptionist. She was a busty redhead with a bubbly personality. "You've got your game on, girl," she said.

"Thanks," Kelly Jo replied.

Lulu dropped her voice. "Didn't work on Brinkley, though, did it?"

Kelly Jo shook her head. She'd been flirting with the hotel general manager for the last few days, testing the waters to see if they could use him as cover to get the room safe master passcode.

"I told you. That man just doesn't cheat. I've done everything except put my hand down his pants."

"Which of the assistant managers do you think is most likely?"

"With access to the passcode? Cassady would be our guy. He's the one the boss paid off to get us our jobs."

"Which one is he?"

"The slick dresser who thinks he's a player."

"The dark-haired guy who's always ogling the waitresses?"

"That's him."

"Couldn't we just pay him for the info?"

"No can do. We have to get the info without him knowing."

"So we need access to his office computer."

"Exactly."

Two couples rolled their bags up to the counter. Lulu and Kelly Jo checked them in and directed them to the elevator.

"How long have you been at this?" Kelly Jo asked.

"A few years. Koenig found me at an escort service. It's the same job, just pays a lot better. What about you?"

"Max and me have been tag-teaming a long time. You and JB together?"

She giggled. "Just between you and me, the boss asked me to take care of him. Didn't want him to get bored and stray. I get something extra in my pay envelope for my trouble."

"Does JB know?"

"He knows what he needs to know. What about your man? He's a handsome devil. Is he available, or are you keeping him for yourself?"

A mom and dad with three children approached the counter. The mom unfolded a paper. "We have a reservation. Peterson."

Kelly Jo input the name into her computer. "James Peterson?"

The woman glanced at her husband, who was trying not to look in Kelly Jo's cleavage. "Uh-huh," he said.

"We have you booked for four days. We've put you poolside, if that's okay?"

MAX, wearing his maintenance uniform and tool belt, got on the service elevator on the twelfth floor. He pressed the basement button. The elevator opened on the eighth. A small Latina in a maid's uniform was navigating a cart piled high with sheets.

"Let me help you with that." He stepped to the side and reached for the cart.

"I'm okay."

"It's no trouble." He pulled the cart onto the elevator. "You going all the way down?"

"*Si.*" She studied his face. "You're new."

He nodded.

"Don't let a supervisor catch you where you're not supposed to be. They'll fire you just like that." She snapped her fingers.

"As long as I'm wearing this toolbelt, I think I'll be all right."

The elevator opened. He helped her navigate the cart into the hallway. "Be seeing you."

She pushed the cart toward the laundry. He strolled off in the other direction to the maintenance shop. JB was standing at a workbench, scrolling down the screen of a computer tablet. He wore a fat man's beard, and his glasses were always sliding down his nose. "Hey."

"Hey," JB said. "It was just like I told you, wasn't it?"

"Yeah. Nobody's coming or going from the roof. Spectacular view, though."

"Whatever. I don't know why the boss brought you two in. There's not that much to do."

"Like I said, we're old hands at this kind of work. Looks like you need a little help with the manager anyway."

"Lulu can handle it."

"On the big day, two people can't get through that many rooms, even with the room keycard and room safe passcode."

Just then, Kevin Crier, the maintenance manager, came barreling into the shop, his bald head glistening with sweat. "What are you two doing hanging around here? There's a blocked toilet in room 1026. Grab the plumbing cart and get up there."

Max found the plumbing cart among the various tool carts parked against the back wall of the shop, pulled it out, and followed JB back down the hall to the service elevator. When the door opened, he pushed the cart all the way to the back wall. JB pressed the tenth-floor button.

"So, Lulu," Max said. "How long have you known her?"

"I met her here."

"She's got some dangerous curves, amigo. You hitting that?"

JB gave him a dirty look. "Shut your mouth."

"I'm just saying—"

"She's my girl. You stick to your own."

"No offense meant."

"I'm not kidding."

Max smiled to himself. JB had so many buttons to push. He was going to be easy to manage. The elevator door opened. "Sorry we got off on the wrong foot."

"We don't need to talk. Let's just fix the toilet."

LATER, after supper, Max and Kelly Jo, dressed as guests rather than employees, were walking the viewing path through the woods at the back of the island. Up ahead was the rock outcropping with the bench that offered an unobstructed view of the bay. A man and a woman were sitting there, kissing passionately. Max and Kelly Jo walked off the path down a narrow dirt trail and ended up sitting on a boulder, out of sight of the lovebirds. A sailboat was tacking back and forth across the bay.

"Lulu was right," Kelly Jo said. "The manager won't play. So we're going to work on Cassady."

Max peered down the rocky slope to the water. No trail and no beach. "I'm sure you'll get it done. No way to bring in gear here."

"Probably a better spot by the old cabins to the east."

"We'll have to figure out what they're using them for."

"What do you think of JB?"

"He knows maintenance work, which is a plus. And he must know the computer stuff or Koenig wouldn't have brought him in. But he's no grifter. I pissed him off without even trying."

"Koenig is paying Lulu to fuck him."

Max chuckled. "He thinks they're in love."

"She asked if you were available."

He squeezed her hand. "We're not going to have any trouble keeping them off balance, are we?"

They heard the couple walking back toward the hotel. "Sounds like they're ready for round two," Max said. "Let's get a view from the top."

Up at the bench, they could see over the entire back third of the island. It was all steep, and mostly rocky, although there was a heavily treed section that could be hiding a trail. "Can't see the cabins from here," Kelly Jo said.

"Or the VIP marina."

"But it's got to be down below the trees over there, because there's the electrical tower."

Max gestured at the water in the distance. "You can see any boat crossing from the city to the marina."

"Yeah, but I wouldn't want to get caught up here hoping to escape." She turned back toward the path. "You ready to go back to the Treasure Cove?"

"You really do like that old tourist court."

"I do. I love all that touristy kitsch down by the old amusement park. Reminds me of the woodsy place we hid out at after the Houston job. Remember all the fun we had there?"

"I could never forget. But I want to time-off the rent-a-cops first. They should be rounding the gazebo behind the patio restaurant in thirty minutes."

"You sure?" She stood up on her toes to kiss him. "I'm feeling a little frisky."

He put his arms around her and whispered in her ear. "Give me thirty minutes and I'll make up the time on the drive."

"You think so?"

"I'll run every red light."

"You're on."

THE NEXT DAY, Max worked second shift, so midmorning he went out to Solomon Island posing as a day gambler: jeans, golf shirt, blue blazer, and panama hat. Once he was through the metal detector at the ferry dock, he bought a coffee at the Caffeination coffee shop next to Island T-Shirts and across the circle drive from the casino hotel. He stopped at a bench, blew on his coffee, and scanned the distance as if he were contemplating his day. A middle-aged man wearing shorts and a short-sleeve shirt came out of the front of the hotel, putting his room keycard in his shirt pocket. Max tossed his coffee into a trash-can, set a course to intercept the man, striding along as if he were late for something. Just as the man rounded a luggage cart, Max banged into the man's shoulder and lifted his room keycard. "Wow, so sorry. I've got to look where I'm going," he said.

"No problem," the man replied.

The man continued toward the marina. Max slowed his pace and turned toward the vehicle rental kiosk. Just another vacationer. Two men and a woman dressed in hotel uniforms were working at the kiosk, the men standing to one side, the woman inputting something on a computer tablet. He studied them for a moment. He hadn't seen any of them before.

He rapped his knuckles on the counter. "How you doing?"

The woman looked up expectantly. "Yes, sir?"

"I want to rent a golf cart."

"Certainly. Have you got your room keycard?"

He handed her the man's keycard.

She swiped it. "Thank you, Mr. Charles. Do you want that charged to your room?"

"Yes, thank you."

She handed back the keycard. "Hey, Jimmy, can you pull up a golf cart for Mr. Charles?"

The younger of the two men nodded and walked off into the parking area. A few minutes later he came back driving a golf cart. "Please stay on the cart paths, sir."

"You bet," Max said.

He drove down the path along the east side of the island. There were dunes to his left with periodic walking paths that led to the swimming beach. To the right was a narrow savanna that transitioned into the woods that covered the back of the island. A couple of teenagers in swimwear, towels around their necks, rode past him on bikes going back toward the hotel. Beyond the dunes was a group of dilapidated, tin-roofed cabins that were probably the employee housing for the casino back before the hotel and the new ferry. Max pulled his cart off the path and strolled down among the cabins. At the first cabin he came to, the porch leaned severely away from the front wall, one of the windows was boarded up, and the screen door hung off the hinges. He peeked in a dirty window. Old furniture was stacked in the center of the room. The other cabins were more of the same, except some were stacked with boxes, while others contained pieces of equipment that looked like they were being kept for spare parts.

On the other side of the cabins, the beach was pea gravel right down to a broken-down boat dock. A single light pole stood next to the closest dock post. Max studied the gravel and the hardpacked sand exposed by low tide. No tracks or footprints would show here. At the top of the light pole, he saw a surveillance camera. Was there power? Was the camera working? Was this area the ghost town it appeared to be? Or was that just what any guests who strayed here were supposed to think? Was this the landing place for items that were too sensitive to bring in via the VIP marina? If that was the case, there'd be no surveillance. But if this place was as deserted as it appeared to be, maybe this was the place to land Koenig's gear, or maybe he and Kelly Jo could board a boat here if they needed to. He could have JB check to see if the surveillance was working and knock it out.

When he got back to the cart path, a security officer on a moped was stopped by the golf cart. "Hello," Max said.

"Hello, sir," the officer said. "I was wondering if this cart was abandoned."

"No, I'm just sightseeing. Taking a break from the casino."

"You want to stay on the path, sir. Some of these areas aren't safe to explore. Derelict buildings, sinkholes, even old blasting caps—it's just better to stay on the path. You'll get the best views, too."

"Thanks for the info."

"You bet."

The security officer drove off down the path. Max got back in the golf cart. He continued along the path into the woods, up the low hill to behind the hotel. Families were sitting out at umbrella tables by the pool, eating brunch. To his left was the footpath that led through the woods to the rocky outcropping overlooking the bay. The security officer was standing near the gazebo. Max gave him a nod as he drove by. Down the hill he could see the landscapers' garages and beyond them the VIP marina with its boat slips. Everything was just as it should be. There were no mob guys in their loud clothes looking vaguely intimidating. The security people, uniform and plainclothes, all seemed completely professional. He followed the path around to the front of the hotel. In the week he'd been here, he hadn't seen anything to indicate that the casino was mobbed up.

He returned the golf cart to the vehicle rental kiosk. The young woman was gone. He went in the service entrance at the side of the hotel, took the stairs down to the basement, and went into the locker room, where he changed into his maintenance uniform. On his way to the maintenance shop, the woman from the kiosk came out of the women's locker room dressed in her street clothes. She stopped in front of him, a quizzical look on her face. "Have we met?"

He smiled. "I get that all the time. I look like everybody. I'm Max."

"I'm Molly."

"See you around, Molly."

JB was in the maintenance shop. He had a vacuum cleaner up on a workbench, the bottom open to expose the brush roller and the belt. "You just now getting here?"

"Yeah."

"We're got five vacuums to service, so pick one up. The tag will tell you what the problem is."

"The maids don't change the belts?"

"The maids only empty the bag."

Max set the nearest vacuum cleaner down on the other work-bench. The intake was clogged. "This place seem mobbed up to you?"

JB looked up. "What are you talking about?"

"This place is supposed to be a money laundry. We're supposed to be here to rob the laundry."

"Keep your voice down. That's above my pay grade. The boss knows what he's doing. He always does. I've never been busted and I've never been shorted working with him."

"I'm just saying—"

"Don't make waves. Do your part. Let other folks do their part. Okay?"

"Okay."

Koenig, Raymond, and Hernandez were sitting at a table away from the stage in the Shoot 'Em Up Gentleman's Club. The bartenders wore golf shirts, and the waitresses wore tight black T-shirts with tiny skirts and colored panties. The place was two-thirds empty and a second-string dancer was working the pole as if they'd only just been introduced. Hernandez shook the ice in his drink. Raymond gestured to their waitress for another round.

"You happy with your accommodation?" Koenig asked.

"It'll do."

"Only neighborhood with Latinos. Didn't want you to stick out," Raymond said.

"Where are you at with your crew?" Koenig continued.

"Still waiting on two guys. Otherwise, we're good."

"Tell me about the demolition guy."

"Ex Special Forces. I've worked with him before. And he's never been arrested."

"He's going to be with you."

"So what are we going to do?"

"Your crew will rob the Solomon Island casino."

"Don't they have a private SWAT team on site?"

"Yes."

"So we're not robbing the casino. That's just a diversion. What's Raymond's crew doing?"

"I haven't told him yet."

They stopped talking while the waitress set down their drinks.

"You haven't told him yet? You expect me to believe that?" Hernandez asked.

"I don't know any more than you," Raymond said.

"Rest assured," Koenig continued. "No matter what happens, you'll make twenty-five grand. And you'll know all the details in plenty of time. Other people are in place, making preparation. No one gets to know everything until it's time. Just make sure that your people can work together under pressure."

Two DAYS LATER, at four in the afternoon, Kelly Jo and Lulu were moving down the employees-only hallway behind the reception counter, heading toward the assistant managers' offices. They'd been stalking Johnny Cassady, learning the details of his schedule, and now they were ready to act. Lulu unbuttoned the top two buttons on her blouse. "You want to fuck him?"

"Cassady? Sure," Kelly Jo replied. "He's pretty enough. His hands are clean. Why? You want to fuck him?"

"I could do with a change."

"Girlfriend, the casino is full of horny men."

"I don't want JB to get jealous. He pouts, gets grouchy. Then I have to turn on the make-up sex. Way too much effort for what he delivers."

"Want to work it like the first reel of a porno?"

"Sounds good."

They came around the corner. Johnny Cassady, slim-cut suit and an expensive haircut, was standing in the door to his office. He grinned. "Ladies."

Kelly Jo and Lulu gave each other a flirty smile, and then Lulu was on him. She kissed him and pushed him back into his office. Kelly Jo shut the door.

"Mr. Cassady, I think we're all off duty at the same time," Lulu purred.

"Whoa," he said, "What's going on here?"

Lulu hiked up her skirt. She wasn't wearing panties. "It's your lucky day."

Cassady glanced at Kelly Jo. She was smiling and nodding. She came around behind him and started pulling his suit coat down his shoulders. He shrugged it off. He put his hands on Lulu's hips.

She stepped just out of reach. "Isn't there a bed in the First Aid office? Hasn't the nurse practitioner left for the day?"

"We don't want to get caught," he said.

"Then we better get moving."

"Safer here."

"But not enough room for both of us."

Kelly Jo slipped her hand down the back of his pants. "It's just a few doors down."

His head swiveled from Kelly Jo to Lulu. "Okay. Let's go."

Lulu opened the door and glanced down the hall both ways. "All clear."

They rushed down the hall, the three of them moving as one. As soon as the First Aid office door shut, JB came out of the supply room across the hall and went into Cassady's office. He sat down behind the desktop computer, pressed the power button, rubbed his hands together while the screen came up, and hacked his way in. A few moments later, he was scrolling through files. And there it was. Not even encrypted. The room safe master passcode. He took out his phone and speed dialed Max. "You ready?"

Max was in a fifth-floor room, replacing lightbulbs. "Just a second." He opened the closet and knelt down in front of the safe. "Go."

JB told him the passcode. He pressed the buttons on the keypad of the safe. The safe made its reassuring open sound. "We're good to go."

JB shut down Cassady's computer, slipped out of the office, and took the stairs to the basement.

Meanwhile, in the First Aid office, Lulu and Kelly Jo had Cassady on his back on the treatment bed, his shirt open and his pants around his ankles, Lulu riding him like a bronco buster while Kelly Jo kissed him and rubbed his chest. Kelly Jo felt her phone vibrate. She glanced at the screen. Text message from Max. *All done.*

She pinched Lulu's leg to get her attention and then nodded. Lulu nodded back. She finished Cassady and rode hard to her own orgasm. Then she lay on his chest, out of breath, smiling her satisfaction.

"Oh boy," Cassady said. "That was crazy."

Kelly Jo stepped to the door. "Shush."

Cassady glanced over at her. Lulu climbed off him and started buttoning her blouse.

"I thought I heard someone," Kelly Jo said.

Cassady pulled up his pants. "Jesus. I've got to get out of here."

Cassady and Lulu finished dressing while Kelly Jo pretended to be listening at the door.

"Ladies," Cassady said, "that was really something. Maybe we could get together when we have a little more time."

Lulu fluffed her hair. "Are you talking dinner before dessert?"

"Absolutely." He looked from Lulu to Kelly Jo. "Let's just keep this on the down low around here."

Lulu and Kelly Jo nodded. "Of course," Kelly Jo said. "None of us needs any workplace drama."

"I'm glad you understand." He opened the door and glanced down the hall. "Give me a few minutes' head start. Just in case someone comes around the corner."

He shut the door as he left. Lulu turned to Kelly Jo. "Am I all put together?"

"You look great."

"We'll tell the guys that you fucked him, if that's okay."

"Fine with me."

Lulu looked at the treatment bed. "Should we change the sheet?"

"No. If the nurse practitioner reports it, it just means we won't have to fuck Cassady here again."

"How incriminating do you think the hallway surveillance camera is going to be?"

"For us? There's no reason for management to check it until after the robbery. For him? If they do look back this far, he's screwed."

Then Lulu and Kelly Jo started laughing, their hands over their mouths, laughing so hard that the tears started from their eyes.

"Oh God," Lulu said. She blew her nose. "Cassady is one clueless idiot."

Kelly Jo blotted the tears from her face. "Glad there are so many of them. Makes our work easier. Let's get out of here."

ON RIDGEWAY AVENUE, in a one-story rental house in a suburban neighborhood, Koenig and Raymond walked through the house with the rental agent. It was an open floor plan with a kitchen island separating the kitchen from the living-room dining-room area. A four-chair dining room table sat near the island and two sofas faced a flat screen TV mounted on the living room wall.

"Is this a quiet neighborhood?" Koenig asked. "The kind of neighborhood where people keep to themselves?"

The rental agent, a chatty grandma in a fitted suit, smiled. "The neighbors are hardly home."

"Let's see the basement."

She led the way. The basement was unfinished concrete with two lightbulbs hanging from the joists and a toilet and sink set in one corner. "Not much to see."

They went back upstairs. Koenig looked out the back window, across the backyard to a trampoline in the yard across the way.

"Oh," the rental agent said, "that's a leftover. The kids over there are all in high school now."

"We'll take it," Koenig said.

"Fully furnished?"

"Of course."

THE NEXT DAY Max and Kelly Jo were both off work, so they decided to scout the casino again. Max put on a little fake mustache and wrap-around sunglasses to go with his Panama hat and cargo shorts. Kelly Jo wore a long dress with sleeves, a summer hat with a huge brim, and cats-eye glasses. At 11:00 a.m. they came off the ferry through the tourist metal detectors, walked up the hill and straight into the casino entrance. It was the usual sort of interior: cashiers along one wall, slot machines all through the middle, blackjack, poker, and craps grouped in the back. No windows, no clocks, and so many surveillance cameras that they weren't worth counting. The space was already jammed with people. They moved along like they were older than they really were, maybe just a touch confused. They stopped at a bar and ordered a drink.

"How many supervisors do you think?" Max asked.

"No more than usual. And no more than last time."

"I know. And the security officers aren't hiding."

"And Cassady, the assistant manager, he's not mob material. He's just a regular old vanilla hospitality manager."

Max sipped his beer. "So how is this place a money laundry?"

"If that's not the job, what is the job?"

"We're collecting the info to rob the rooms. We know that for a fact. But there's nothing that anyone would put in a room safe that's valuable enough to go to this much trouble. So that has to be the side hustle."

"Or just more misdirection," Kelly Jo said.

"Exactly."

"And robbing the casino is a nonstarter."

He nodded. "Gates at the cashiers' windows. Private security right here on the island. Wouldn't even need a minute hand to time off the armed-response team."

"And if miracles on top of miracles you open the vault—"

"Can't be done."

"But if—that's all I'm saying. You still can't get off the island using the ferry," Kelly Jo said.

"You'd get trapped in the kill box."

"Or they'd hold the ferry until the police arrived."

"So whatever the real game is, you have to take it off by boat," Max said.

"Or helicopter."

"And either way, there is no room for the so-called diversion crew that is supposed to pretend to rob the casino. They'd all have to be left behind."

"Dead or in jail."

"It just doesn't make sense."

"Not yet."

They walked out of the casino and down toward the VIP marina. "Lots of places to land a helicopter," she said. "Behind the hotel, right down in front, back by the cabins on the east side."

"You could hover it over the top of the hotel, so long as you didn't set down."

A number of pleasure boats were moored in the marina. One unarmed security guard stood in a kiosk by the walkway. "There's no real security down here," Kelly Jo said.

"Management isn't worried about the VIPs. Besides, the water is just too shallow for a large craft. The biggest boat out here, you might cram ten people aboard."

They sat down on a bench overlooking the water. "What about hijacking the rental pontoon boat?"

Max shook his head. "Not fast enough. You'd be chased down by a speed boat."

Four young men, drinks in hand, sauntered toward them, talking loudly about their afternoon plans. One of the men, his golf shirt partially untucked, elbowed his nearest friend and then pointed at Max and Kelly Jo. He dug into his pocket and came out with a wad of wrinkled cash. "Hey, lady, what do you want for that hat?"

His buddy put one hand over his face and started sniggering. The other two guys turned to see what was going on.

Kelly Jo smiled vacantly. "My hat's not for sale, young man."

Max cut in. "Have you got nothing better to do than bother a lady?"

"I wasn't talking to you," the young man said. "Twenty dollars. I'll give you twenty dollars."

One of the other guys stepped into the middle with his hands in surrender mode. "Sorry. Don't pay any attention to him." He turned to the guy holding the wad of cash. "You want to get us kicked out of here? Let's go."

"I'm just asking."

They led him away, his other friend still laughing. They took the path down among the boats. Max shook his head. "Casino resorts."

"Exactly," Kelly Jo said. "Lots of employees, lots of drunks, lots of distracted people. Koenig's bringing in his people on the ferry. On Saturday. This place will be jammed with visitors. If there's enough confusion, most of his people could just blend back in."

"So all you need is transportation for the people who are carrying the haul. Duffel bags of money? Six guys? Jewels? Less than that. What if he's just tapping into the computer and moving money electronically? Two or three guys could just run down here to a boat like they're afraid for their lives and voila! They're gone."

"So we don't care about the casino."

"No, we don't," Max said. "But we do need to know what's happening on the island. We have to land Koenig's gear—best spot we've found is at the east cabins. And we have to have a place to meet our partner."

"There's got to be a place at the back of the island. We just haven't found it yet. Who're you thinking about bringing in to help?"

"Anders lives near here. He knows weapons, cars, and he can drive a boat."

"He's not too smart."

"But he can follow directions."

"You're right. And he's easy to work with."

"That's because he's got a crush on you."

"Please—"

Max chuckled. "Don't deny it."

Kelly Jo stood up. "We done here?"

"You trying to change the subject?"

"Yes."

"Let's do another count on the security guards around the building."

At 1:00 p.m., Lulu and JB sat at a picnic table in the employees' area by the landscapers' garages, finishing their lunch. The other tables were empty, except for a group of maids seated at the only table under the shade tree. "Did you see Max and Kelly Jo earlier?" Lulu asked.

"Max isn't working today."

"Kelly Jo, either. They were dressed up—in disguises. I saw them walk by the front of the hotel going toward the marina."

"Really? You sure it was them?"

"Definitely."

"What were they doing?"

"I don't know."

"You think we're fooling them?" JB asked.

"I'm pretty sure she's buying the jealousy story I'm selling."

"How so?"

"She lied about fucking Cassady to cover up for me."

"True. And he went all defensive when I snapped at him for asking about you."

"So there you have it," Lulu said.

"The boss said they're master manipulators. That we can't believe anything about them."

"Well, we're master manipulators, aren't we? The boss chose us to close the deal. So he must believe we can do it."

"We can't get overconfident. We need to keep them off balance until we've got all the valuables from the safes," JB said.

"The codebook, you mean?"

"Well, yeah. But that's the boss's. I still want to empty as many of the other safes as we can."

"To share?"

"To keep for ourselves. It'll be a tidy little bonus. We can blame the loss on Max and Kelly Jo after we kill them."

Lulu wrapped the remaining third of her sandwich in its wrapper. "Why do we have to kill them? That just seems like extra risk."

"Don't worry about it. I'll take care of it. You just have to help me wrangle them. Do your talking, make them feel comfortable. I'll do the rest."

"Okay, I can do that."

"That's all I'm asking." He crumpled up his sandwich wrapper and shoved it into his empty cup. "I've got to get back. Crier has been on the warpath lately."

A FEW HOURS LATER, Max and Kelly Jo were on the ferry back to Bathsheba City, sitting out in the open at the front, hiding in plain sight. Even though a heavy bank of clouds was rolling in, most of the other passengers were on the upper deck. Tourists were taking pictures of the island and the Bathsheba City marina, where a crowd was already waiting to make the trip to the island. Max's phone rang. It was Zeb, a criminal supply contractor they used when they didn't use Billy. Weapons, information, criminal contacts—he was the one-stop shop.

"Hey, buddy, what's up?"

"I did that checking," Zeb said. "Appears Solomon Island is a Smithson laundry. Drugs, gambling, chop-shop money come in on different days in different amounts."

"No way to know ahead of time?"

"Money is coming in all the time. What amount on what day? You'd have to be involved pretty high up."

"Thanks."

He put away his phone. "Things just got complicated." He leaned over to Kelly Jo and whispered what he learned.

"So it may be as advertised," Kelly Jo said.

"Maybe. I still don't believe it. Too much effort. Too many ways to go wrong."

"But we can't count it out."

"No, we can't."

They sat silently for the rest of the ferry ride. They were the first ones off the ferry and into the parking lot. As they crossed the asphalt to their car, Kelly Jo said, "What about Lulu and JB? Do you think they are who they appear to be?"

Max pressed the fob to unlock their Cadillac. "I don't know. We know she's a hustler, and he's a computer guy, but the rest of it? If they aren't who they seem to be, they know what they're doing. Either way, we're going to play along and not let our guard down."

They got into the Cadillac and headed back toward the Treasure Cove Tourist Court. Max's Koenig phone rang. He put it on speaker.

"Yeah?"

"How are you doing, my boy?"

"Just fine."

"I hear from our mutual friends that you all have found out everything we need to know for the big day."

"Yes, indeed."

"Do you know where we'll bring our gear in?"

"Nothing's ideal, but the best spot is at the old cabins on the east side."

"When?"

"We want to avoid discovery, so this is last minute."

"I agree, but not too last minute."

"I'll keep an eye out to make sure it's safe. Then I'll be in touch."

"Good enough." Koenig ended the call.

Kelly Jo pulled into the left turn lane at the traffic light. "So he really does need the gear."

"He's following his MO. Every group is compartmentalized. But it does look like he's assembling a large team. He probably really is planning to use the casino robbery as a diversion. And Lulu and JB are probably really planning to rob the room safes. But the real score? We still don't have any idea, so we've got to take every precaution."

3

THE COUNTDOWN

The next evening, Max and Kelly Jo were waiting for Anders in a Caffeination coffee shop at the strip mall near Bathsheba Community College. Most of the tables were taken up with students working on laptops, but they found a table back near the restroom. Anders raised a hand when he spotted them. He was a small, wiry man with a red-gray ponytail. He wore garage coveralls with the name *Jones* embroidered on the breast pocket.

He smiled as he pulled out a chair to sit down. "The mister and the missus. Good to hear from you. How you been?"

"It's all good," Kelly Jo said.

"Got a little something you might want to join in on," Max said.

"I was hoping. Give me the outline."

"Not sure how the money is going to go. We could guarantee ten grand or you could come in for a fifth share."

"Which could be what?"

"Maybe as much as thirty-two thousand."

"Now you're talking."

"No guarantees."

"In this life? Nothing's guaranteed except dying alone."

"So you're in?"

"I've never seen you set up a second-rate job."

"There's a lot of ifs in this one. We're doing something out on Solomon Island that involves some other players. You're part of our backup plan. We're going to need a boat, a clean car, a storage locker, safe house, and heavy gear."

"When?"

"Nine days, more or less. Right now we're planning for the Saturday."

"I can do that. What kind of gear we talking about?"

"Automatic rifles big enough to scare, heavy bulletproof vests in case we need to use them. Here's a list. Plus the breakdown for the other items."

"No problem. The expenses come out of the pot?"

"Always." Max pushed an envelope of money across the table. "That should get you started."

Anders glanced in the envelope. "I'm guessing you needed all this stuff lined up yesterday?"

Max nodded.

Anders turned to Kelly Jo. "Always a pleasure to see you." He reached over the table to Max. They shook hands. "The phone number you gave me good?"

Max nodded.

"I'll be in touch."

They finished their coffees while they gave Anders a few minutes to drive away.

THE NEXT DAY, at the Ridgeway Avenue house, Hernandez backed into the garage with a truckload of constructions materials. Day laborers he'd hired from the Home Depot parking lot that morning were down in the basement building a room in the corner that contained the toilet and sink. They had already framed up the walls and were setting the electrical outlets in preparation for the drywall. He called down the stairs to them. Two men came up, grabbed a sheet of drywall, and carried it downstairs, where they pushed it up against the inside wall of the new room. Another man started screwing the drywall in place. As soon as he was done, a man with a saw cut out a spot for a window, while the first two men went upstairs for another sheet of drywall.

Raymond stood in the middle of the space, supervising. "It doesn't have to be pretty, but it does have to be strong."

His cellphone rang. "How's it going?" Koenig asked.

"Speeding along. We're not taping the drywall, so we'll be painting tomorrow."

"Excellent."

"But what's it for? What does it have to do with our plan?"

"You know I'm not going to tell you yet. Don't think too hard about it. It's just part of our insurance policy." Koenig ended the call.

Raymond went upstairs into the kitchen. Hernandez stood at the sink, drinking a glass of water. "These guys are doing great."

Hernandez set his glass on the counter. "What did I tell you? It's easy to find good workers if you know where."

Raymond glanced out into the living room. Everyone else was working in the basement. "So what's your angle?"

"What do you mean?"

"I know you're not working for twenty-five grand."

Hernandez stuck his thumbs into his belt. "You got something to say?"

"We could go in together. I'm not greedy. We could even kick more money down to the other guys, if that's what you want."

"You think there's that much money that's not the casino?"

"Has to be. There's too many moving parts on this job for it to be pocket change."

"How do I know this isn't a test? That Koenig isn't just wanting to know whether he needs to kill me instead of pay me?"

"You've worked on four jobs for the old man."

Hernandez nodded.

"How many people ended up being paid?"

"Not very many."

"So you're good at staying out of the way at the right time and also knowing where the real meet-up is going to take place," Raymond said.

"Easy to do if you're holding the score."

"But you won't be holding the score this time. I will."

"So why do you want to help me?"

"Because you're going to try to steal the score, just like me. I'm the closest to Koenig. I'm going to know all the details that he's willing to share. But I need a partner to close the deal. I can't be everywhere at once. And if Koenig gets shy with me, he's going to have to rely on somebody. I'm betting that somebody is you. Between the two of us, we'll know everything. That makes us natural partners."

"Okay, *hermano*, if we're partners, you tell me who we're planning to hold in the cell we're building in the basement."

"I don't know yet."

"I see."

"But as soon as I do know, you will. Just like anything else I find out. I share with you. You share with me. Partners."

Hernandez nodded. "Okay, then. Partners."

OVER THE NEXT WEEK, Cassady pestered Lulu and Kelly Jo for another threesome, this time at his apartment in town, but they kept making promises and excuses. Max and Kelly Jo continued to walk the island whenever they had the chance, but they didn't notice anything that would help them figure out what was really happening on Saturday. JB continued being taciturn and argumentative, and Lulu kept up her charm offensive, neither set of behaviors causing Max or Kelly Jo to let down their guard.

Finally, on the Wednesday before the Saturday heist, as Max and Kelly Jo drove back to the tourist court after supper, Max took out the Koenig phone. "It's time to land Koenig's gear. It doesn't make any sense to put it off any longer."

"We could still run," Kelly Jo said. "We don't know what the job is. We don't know how much danger we're in."

"We're in the maximum amount of danger. That's the amount we're always in when we don't know how much danger we're in."

"Like I said, we could still run."

"Don't you want to know what this job is about? JB doesn't know. Lulu doesn't know."

"That's because they're trusting Koenig."

"On Saturday we've got plenty of cover. Solomon Island will be crawling with people. Anders will be there with the boat. If it all goes to hell, we'll get away. That's when it'll be time to run."

"You always have to cut it close."

"That's where the money is."

"Okay. I'll go that far. But remember what you promised me."

"I remember. You say run, we run. But I still think we can screw him."

"But Saturday is the line."

"It's the line."

"Make the call."

He put his phone on speaker and dialed JB. "Hey, JB."

"What's up?"

"You know the old dock on the east side of the island?"

"Yeah?"

"There's a surveillance camera there. Can you turn it off?"

"Why?"

"Just something for the boss. Turn it off and make sure it stays off."

"Okay, if it's for the boss."

"Thanks. Can you do that now?"

"Give me five minutes."

Max ended the call and called Koenig.

"Kid, what's up?"

"It's time to land your gear."

"I was beginning to wonder. Still on the east side?"

"Yes."

"You've checked it out?"

"JB is turning off the surveillance camera."

"Meet us there."

"I'll ride with you."

"Come down to the B&B marina. Raymond will meet you at the gate."

Max put his phone away.

"You're going with them?" Kelly Jo asked.

"They're not going to go if I don't go."

"They might kill you."

"No, it's not his style. He hasn't gotten enough use out of me yet. If he's going to kill us, he'll do it on the day of."

"What a comforting thought."

They took Kennedy Boulevard downtown, skirted the stop-and-go traffic in the old port commercial zone with its restaurants and boutique shops, and came to the marina through the old warehouse district. Once they'd gotten through the downtown traffic, all the traffic lights were green. Kelly Jo stopped in the parking lot directly in front of the chain-link fence that guarded the B&B marina. Raymond was waiting at the gate. "Go somewhere else," Max said. "I'll call you when I get back." He took his .38 out of his jacket pocket and laid it on the seat.

"I don't have to tell you to be careful."

"No, but I like it when you do."

Max stepped out of the car. Raymond unlocked the gate and held it open. "You carrying?"

"Why? We getting in a gunfight?"

"Follow me."

They walked along the wharf until they reached a weekender yacht. Two Latinos stood on the deck. "Let's get underway," Raymond said.

One of the Latinos climbed into the cockpit and started the motor.

"You know where we're going?" Max asked.

"Yeah. I've scouted the island. And we've got a good night. Plenty of moon."

"How much gear do we have to unload?"

"Have a look." He led Max to the cabin door and opened it. At least eight boxes, some as large as four feet by two feet, were stacked in the space.

"Not too bad."

They stood in silence on the deck as they wove their way through the nearby boats to open water and motored across the bay to Solomon Island. As they approached the island, they turned off their running lights, stayed well away from the VIP marina, rounded the back of the island in the dark, and approached the broken-down dock by the cabins, navigating by moonlight.

"The pole light is out," Raymond said.

"Surveillance camera as well," Max replied.

Raymond got out a pair of night-vision binoculars and scanned the beach and cabins. "All clear."

They motored slowly toward the shore until they felt the hull touch bottom. They were about ten feet from the beach. "What's up?" Raymond asked the pilot.

"Low tide," he said.

Raymond looked over the side of the yacht. "Guess we have to hump the gear in. Where are we taking the boxes?" Raymond asked.

"I'll show you. No need to go emptyhanded," Max said. "How deep is the water?"

"Four feet," one of the Latinos said.

"At least it's calm."

Max took off his jacket and climbed down into the sea. The cold water lapped against his chest. One of the Latinos handed down a box. He shifted it onto his shoulder and walked it out onto the pea gravel. Raymond was behind him with another box.

"You could have sent one of the guys," Max said.

"I have to see the spot myself."

They carried the boxes across the gravel to a cabin that Max knew already contained other boxes. Max picked the lock. "We place our boxes around the side, where they can't be seen through the windows."

Raymond nodded. He took a penlight from his shirt pocket to

light their way inside. Several large mover's boxes were stacked six feet high in the middle of the room. They stacked their boxes behind them.

When they got back to the shore, there were two large boxes on the gravel and the Latinos were carrying more through the surf. Max and Raymond picked up a long box between them and carried it back to the cabin. They went back and forth twice more before the Latinos were on the beach helping them. One more trip, and they were done.

Raymond shined his light on the hard-packed sand. "What do we do about the footprints?"

"High tide will take care of that," Max said. "The rest is gravel."

They waded back to the yacht and climbed up the ladder. "Let's go," Raymond said. The pilot backed the yacht off the sand and turned to leave.

"When will they fix the light and the camera?" Raymond asked.

"They won't." Max replied. "Not before Saturday. JB will make sure of that."

"You've done good work here."

"When I'm paid to do a job, I do it right."

Everyone was quiet as they crossed the bay back at the B&B marina, where the pilot pulled back into the slip they'd come out of. "You know your way out," Raymond said.

Max climbed down onto the dock and headed for the gate. His shoes squelched as he walked and his wet pants stuck to his legs. He turned up the collar on his jacket. There were only five cars in the parking lot. All empty. There was no one in sight, no one watching him, no surveillance cameras—at least none he could see. He crossed the parking lot and walked over one block before he called Kelly Jo.

"Hey."

"Hey."

"You can pick me up on Hatcher Boulevard. I'll be on the south side, walking toward Industrial Street."

"I'm on my way."

He'd walked three blocks before Kelly Jo drove up beside him, the Cadillac's flashers pulsing. "You're wet."

"Had to wade." He put his gun back in his pocket.

She pulled away from the curb. "Did you put the gear where you planned?"

"Yeah. Raymond didn't argue at all."

"Koenig wasn't there?"

"Didn't expect him to be."

"So now we're just waiting."

"Waiting and walking the perimeter, looking for tells."

"And waiting on Anders."

"He'll come through. He's got three days."

She turned right at a stop light. "I'd ask you if you wanted to go for a drink, but I guess you'd rather go straight home."

"There's still wine left at the room, isn't there?"

She pulled into the Treasure Cove Tourist Court and parked in front of room 188. A couple were sitting on the Adirondack chairs outside a room down by the office, the red tips of their cigarettes and the silhouettes of their beer bottles visible in their hands. Max and Kelly Jo got out of their car. Max opened the door to their room. The dresser drawers were hanging open, the mattresses were askew on the box springs, and their clothes had been dumped from their roller bags.

Max and Kelly Jo pulled their pistols. Max pushed the door all the way open. The door bounced off the door stop. He stepped in first. No one between the beds. No one in the bathroom. No one in the closet. "All clear."

Kelly Jo shut the door. They stood together, taking in the room, their guns still in their hands. "I don't see anything indicative," she said. "Who do you think it was?"

Max put his pistol in his pocket and put his open roller bag on the bed. "Three options. JB and Lulu. Koenig. Or an unknown player."

She sat on the edge of the bed. "But why? They couldn't learn anything here. And they tipped us that they're looking."

"Which means it wasn't Koenig. His people would have come and gone without leaving a trace. That leaves Lulu and JB, thinking we're as stupid as they are, or, worst option, someone we don't know about."

She put her roller bag on the bed next to his. "And now we have to fold our clothes and find a new motel." She scooped some clothes off the floor and onto the bed next to her roller bag. Max did the same. She folded a blouse and laid it in the bottom of her bag. Max picked up a pair of pants and folded them with the crease. But just before he put them in his bag, he stopped, laid them on the bed, and tapped the edge of Kelly Jo's bag. She glanced up. He held a finger up to his mouth. He found the hotel pad and pen on the dresser and wrote a note. *Did they mess up the room to plant a bug or transmitter in our stuff? We need to check all our gear.*

They felt all over the insides of their roller bags. Clean. They checked each item of clothing—not the pockets, but the seams and cuffs. Nothing. Finally they went through their shower kits, where they found a transmitter hidden in the lining of each bag.

"Very careful," Kelly Jo whispered.

Max nodded. "That's more like Koenig. Room is probably bugged as well."

They left the transmitters in the shower kits. They repacked their roller bags without talking. When they were finished, they rolled their bags out to the Cadillac and drove away from the tourist court. "What a shame," Kelly Jo said. "I really liked that little motel."

"It was bound to happen sooner or later," Max said. He looked out the back window. No one seemed to be following them. "I'm hungry," Max said.

"Drive through?"

"Yeah. Any place is fine with me. What about the Taco Heaven around the corner up here?"

After they went through the drive-through, Kelly Jo drove out to the beltway and got off at the next exit with motels. "Which one? Quality Inn, Budget Inn?"

"How about the Budget Trucker?"

"It's a dump."

"Yep."

They got a room on the ground floor of the Budget Trucker. In the parking lot, pickup trucks were parked in close, while heavier work trucks and semitrucks were parked at the perimeter. They rolled their bags into their room. It smelled of aftershave and Pine Sol. There was a king-size bed with a heavy depression in the middle, a small closet with a few wire hangers, and a mildewed bathroom with cellophane-wrapped plastic cups. A NO SMOKING sign was posted on the back of the door, and the dresser had cigarette burns on the top.

"Home sweet home," Kelly Jo said.

They got their shower kits out of their roller bags, pulled the transmitters, and set them on the shelf in the closet.

"So now they can follow us here," Kelly Jo said.

"Yeah. That's the idea. They'll think we're vulnerable and stupid. We'll have to keep an eye out, just in case they want to bushwhack us, but after the job we'll move to the safe house Anders is setting up and they won't have a clue where we've gone."

MEANWHILE, Raymond looked out the curtains into the front yard of a duplex in a quiet neighborhood. A man and a woman were walking their dogs, the man's dog pulling at its leash while the woman's dog walked close by her feet. Raymond turned back into the dark living room. The local news was on the TV. Light fell in from the kitchen. He took out his phone and speed-dialed Koenig.

"The gear is in place."

"Good," Koenig replied. "Any problems?"

"No, it all went to plan. How did you know he would choose the cabins? We could have just motored up to the marina and left the gear on the boat."

"But then everyone would have to meet at the marina. Too many eyes, too many civilians in the way. That's what the kid would think. He'd rather risk being found by one security guard than enjoy all the extra cover. What have you heard from JB and Lulu?"

"They're ready to go. JB wants to know why they have to wait to kill Max and Kelly Jo."

"Always in a hurry, that one."

"Yeah, I told him to stick with the plan."

"And Max and Kelly Jo's room?"

"Nothing there. They moved to another motel."

"Right now, the kid thinks we don't know he knows about the transmitters."

"You sure he found them?"

"We have to assume so."

"Then why did we plant them?"

"We didn't need to plant them, and we didn't need to toss the room. It's a distraction. I want to keep the kid off balance. The more distractions he has to deal with, the less likely he'll be able to figure out what our real play is before we're gone and he's left holding the bag."

"Okay."

"I've got another one in mind that ought to really wind him up."

"What do you want done?"

"I'm going to have Lulu take care of it. Your end all set?"

"Hernandez's crew is ready, the basement is ready at safe house number one. The only issue is getting the extra vehicle in place. You say go, we could do the job tomorrow."

"Saturday is still the day."

"When will you share the final details?"

"Driving you crazy, isn't it? You'll know on Friday evening. Just you."

"Okay."

Koenig ended the call. Raymond didn't know why Koenig was so tightlipped about the final details. They were robbing a crime family. What could be more dangerous than that? All their people were reliable and professional. Hernandez's crew would create just the amount of chaos necessary to completely intimidate the guests and overcome the security team. When the on-site rapid response arrived with their military gear, and the cops started unloading off the ferry, they'd melt in with the terrified civilians. In the meantime, his team would do the real job, whatever that was, and escape either by helicopter or boat, whichever worked best. Max and Kelly Jo—whoever the hell they were to the boss—would be left to take the fall. And during the confusion, he'd steal the score out from under Koenig and Hernandez—and anyone else who thought they were going to get a taste.

Lulu stood behind the reception counter in the casino hotel. Her shift was almost over. Her legs were tired, and she was hungry. With any luck, JB was off getting drunk somewhere. She was looking forward to putting her feet up and eating a dish of ice cream. The phone rang. "Solomon Islands Casino Resort. How may I help you?"

"Lulu," Koenig said. "It's good to hear your voice. Can you talk?"

She glanced around to make sure no one was close enough to hear her. "Yes, boss."

"How is JB doing?"

"You know JB. Cranky and jealous."

"But he's doing his part?"

"We're all ready."

"You've really gone the extra mile with him."

"Thanks."

"What about Max and Kelly Jo?"

"I think I've got Kelly Jo believing my cover. I got her to lie for me."

"Great."

"But Max is hard to figure, you know? He's a charmer."

"But they're definitely a couple?"

"Yes. They're like married people."

"Can you sow some discord before Saturday? Create some tension between them?"

"That's not much time."

"I know, but that's what I need."

"I'll do my best."

"I know you will. You're going to get an extra half share on this job."

"An extra half share? Thanks, boss."

"You earned it." He ended the call.

Lulu smiled to herself. An extra half share. Well, she had earned it. She deserved combat pay for sleeping with JB. Saturday was three days away. Then she'd be done playing his girlfriend, thank God. But now she needed to focus on Max and Kelly Jo. There was no time to be subtle. She knew exactly what she needed to do to create some friction between them. She wasn't as naturally pretty as Kelly Jo, but she was younger, softer, and rounder. She wouldn't have any trouble getting Max to put his hands on her. She just had to think of a way for Kelly Jo to find out that would drive her over the edge.

4

THE LAST SLEIGHT OF HAND

On Thursday afternoon, Max was in the maintenance shop, sorting through a shelf of paint cans, looking for some touch-up paint for a wall repair when Lulu strolled in. He glanced at her over his shoulder. "If you're looking for JB, he's not here."

Max found the can he was looking for and pulled it off the shelf. Lulu boosted herself up onto a workbench and crossed her legs. "I'm not looking for JB."

He looked her over. The top button of her blouse was undone, and she was pumping her leg in a rhythmically suggestive way. He set the paint can down on the bench beside her. She smiled.

"If your plan is to convince me to fuck you, you're trying too hard. All you had to do was sashay over here and show me the goods."

"Is that right?"

He nodded.

She uncrossed her legs. "What about Kelly Jo?"

"You wanting to include her, or are you planning on telling her?"

"Neither."

He stepped between her legs. "Then we should stop wasting our time."

After Lulu left, he gathered together the paint tray, the small roller, and the paintbrush for the wall repair touchup. Then he stood for a moment looking at the workbench where she'd been sitting. What did she think she was going to accomplish by having sex with him? It was in character for her to try, but it was just a little too strategic, which made it a tell, which meant she wasn't a stupid little nympho. And that meant that everything they thought they knew about her and JB was probably a cover—a cover he could break if he had enough time or interest. But there were only two more days, which meant it was safer to assume they were in on some sort of double cross. So if they even looked at him or Kelly Jo crossways on Saturday, suggested anything the least bit out of the ordinary, he was going to kill them on the spot, just to be on the safe side.

While he was finishing up the paint job on the wall repair in room 836, his smartphone rang. It was Anders. He set the paint roller on the edge of the pan. "Yeah?"

"Mister. I've got what you need. Gear, boat, clean car, safe house, storage locker."

"Where's the car placed?"

"When it's time, it will be up at the state beach north of town."

"Great."

"Where do I bring the boat?"

"I'm still sorting that out. I'll get back with you. Just be ready."

"Okeydokey."

He put away his phone and picked up the paint roller. He was getting that good feeling about this job. Not the feeling that they would make a successful hijack, but the feeling that their process was the correct one—that no matter what happened, they were as ready as they could be. He scrutinized his paint job—the coverage was good —and then feathered in the edges to blend with the rest of the wall. Once the paint was dry, the repair would be invisible. That was the way he always liked to work.

He went back down to the maintenance shop, put away the painting supplies, and washed out the roller and the brush. After he dried his hands, he left the shop, swiped his employee card through the time clock at the end of the hall, changed into street clothes, and walked out of the service entrance. Kelly Jo was already outside, sitting on a bench, playing a game on her smartphone. He sat down beside her. "Lulu came on to me."

Kelly Jo put her phone away. "She texted me a selfie from behind your back."

"I must be slipping. I didn't notice. You sure it was me?"

"I'd know that ass anywhere. Text said you were gentle and sweet."

"That's definitely a provocation. How did you respond?"

"What do you think?"

"You went with the fake *Glad you had a good time.*"

"Just enough irritation in the response to make her think I'm trying to cover up how pissed off I am. Next time we're with them I'm going to be crabby."

"So they're finally trying to play us."

"Not very good at it, are they?"

He chuckled. "No, they're not."

"Think they planted the transmitters?"

"It was half-assed enough to be them, but no, I don't think so. I still think Koenig is trying to mindfuck us. This could just be more of his plan. Let's walk."

They started down the path toward the employee break area by the landscapers' garages. "Anders checked in. He's good to go. But we still need to find a place for him to land on Saturday. A place without any traffic."

"The block of rooms for the birthday party on Saturday has been confirmed. There's not that many of them."

"Really?"

"Yeah. They've reserved a wing, but they're only using six rooms thus far. That's all."

"Then one team would be plenty to take the safes," Max said.

"I know."

"Good thing we have a backup plan. What time is the birthday party?"

"Reservation in a private room at two o'clock."

No one was sitting at the employee picnic tables by the landscapers' garages. They continued around the back of the garages. A dirt path switchbacked down the hill. At the bottom was a rocky beach at a tiny cove. Old fishing line hung in a bush, and a few weathered beer cans littered the gravel. The marina was invisible to the west.

Max skipped a rock across the surf. "No footprints on the path. No recent trash down here."

"It's not ideal, but I think it's the best we're going to find," Kelly Jo said.

Max took her hand. "So we're all ready. If they're robbing the money laundry drop-off, we'll hijack it. If there's some other target, we'll go after it. And either way, we've got Anders and our getaway plan."

"When you first brought this up, I thought we were screwed for sure," Kelly Jo said. "The snake in the Garden of Eden. But I've got to admit, we are set tight."

He kissed her hand. "Have I ever let you down?"

She laughed. "As long as we've been together? You don't even want to go there."

Friday morning, Koenig drove two hours down the freeway to Chester Falls, made his way into a rundown neighborhood of townhouses next to an old shopping mall, and parked in front of a two-chair barber shop that sat on a corner across from a closed-up mom and pop grocery. The white paint on the outside of the shop was peeling, and the windows were dirty, but the glass barber pole sign was brightly lit. Inside, two barbers sat in their barber chairs reading magazines, one a skinny old bald man, the other one a stout man with thinning hair who appeared to be his son. The younger man put down his *Sports Illustrated*.

Koenig shifted his satchel from one hand to the other. "No business?"

The old man glanced over the top of *Guns & Ammo*. "It'll pick up around lunchtime."

"You got what I came for?"

The younger one got out of his chair. "Who are you?"

"Jackie Robinson."

"Really? You don't look a bit like him."

"Don't I know it."

"Come on back."

They walked into the storeroom. There was a toilet and sink, cleaning supplies, and a stack of boxes. "One and one-quarter million is a lot of paper. Took us a while to pull it together."

"But you've got it?"

"Have you got the ten percent?"

"Yes, indeed," Koenig replied. He opened the satchel so that the barber could see inside and then handed it to him.

The barber counted twelve banded bundles of one-hundred dollar bills plus a half bundle, and then pulled one bill at random. He examined it closely, and shined a UV penlight on it. The security thread on the left side glowed pink. "Can't be too careful."

He slid the satchel under the sink before he pulled a large box out of the stack, set it on the floor, and took out two paper grocery bags. Koenig reached into one and took out a bundle of well-used one-hundred dollar bills. He also pulled one at random and examined it. "Nice work. Very precise. And the aging is excellent. How did you get the raised ink?"

"Trade secret."

"And the paper?"

"Not paper. It will pass the ink pen test, but it won't pass the UV light test."

"This is the one and a quarter million?"

"Count the bundles. People always think a million dollars is going to take up more space that it does."

Koenig picked up the bags. "Pleasure doing business with you."

. . .

THAT EVENING at the Bathsheba Fish House, Koenig and Raymond sat together after dinner drinking coffee. Two couples at the table across from them were cracking open crabs on the white paper tablecloth, and two youngsters wearing pirate hats were running toward the front door.

"This is a great fish restaurant," Koenig said.

Raymond shrugged. "If you like fish."

"It's important to have a good meal right before a job. It's a good omen. Gets you ready for what's ahead."

Raymond sipped his coffee and watched the front door.

"Have you briefed everyone?"

"Yeah, all the guys know when and where they need to be in place."

"Even Max?"

"Yes."

"Review it for me."

"We get geared up at the east dock; JB will doublecheck the camera. Hernandez's crew hits the Casino exactly at two thirty. JB, Lulu, Max, and Kelly Jo start on the rooms then."

"That leaves you and your team."

"So where are we going? What are we taking?"

Koenig grinned. "There's no money laundry drop-off on Saturday. Not with Smithson and his family there. But there is a birthday party."

"So what are we stealing? What's so valuable?"

"We're kidnapping Smithson's grandson."

Raymond glanced around as if he were afraid they'd been over-heard. "The grandson?"

"No one will expect it."

"That's for sure."

"You snatch the boy, flash out of there, we ransom him back for two million. It all happens within forty-eight hours."

"So that's what the basement room is for."

"The kid won't see anything."

"Will forty-eight hours be enough time for them to pull the money together?"

"They're not going to the bank."

"It'll be all-out war."

"I hope so. While they're blaming their competitors and each other, we'll be getting away. The key is to move fast. You grab the boy, get to the helicopter. By two forty-five you should be in the air. By three o'clock, Hernandez's crew should be out of the casino and blending in with the guests."

"When do I tell JB and Lulu?"

"You don't. I'm leaving them with Max and Kelly Jo."

"You sure?"

"They've been working there for almost two months. Too many people know their faces. But if they're smart enough to make their way off the island, we'll cut them in." Koenig put some cash on the table. "That will take care of the bill. We'll talk through the details first thing in the morning." He got up from the table.

Raymond watched him walk away. Had Koenig planned this from the very beginning—setting the score so he couldn't be hijacked? Raymond sipped his coffee. He couldn't run with the kid and ransom him himself. With Koenig and Smithson both after him, he'd be dead within days. So he was going to have to bide his time. Wait for the next opportunity. When they traded the kid for the money, he could pull a grab and dash. He'd have to split the score with Hernandez, if he was still alive after tomorrow, but Koenig hadn't exaggerated. This was the score of a lifetime. Half would be plenty.

5

THE HEIST

On Saturday at 11:00 a.m., Hernandez sat on a bench in front of the casino hotel, watching the security checkpoint at the ferry dock. He wore military boots, khaki pants, a loose-fitting jacket, and dark sunglasses. He looked like he was reading something on his phone and enjoying the sun, maybe waiting for his family to join him, but he was counting off his and Raymond's crew members as they passed through security and disappeared into the throng of vacationers and day guests. So far, so good. After he spotted their final man coming up the hill, he turned toward Raymond, who was standing outside the Caffeination coffee shop, and gave him a quick nod. Then he strolled off toward the east path that led down to the deserted cabins at the old dock.

Raymond, dark suit, no tie, meandered into the hotel lobby. Lulu and Kelly Jo were working the reception counter, where several guests stood in line to check in. He turned into the restaurant, where the buffet brunch was still being served. He'd received the hotel plans from JB, but there really wasn't any substitute for walking off the ground yourself. He wandered through the tables as if he were looking for friends, then cut out a side exit into the hallway where the party rooms were located. He stopped in front of the room marked

"Smithson Birthday." One table, eight chairs, eight place settings. Lulu and Kelly Jo's info appeared to be correct. He continued down the hall to the double doors that led to the kitchen and peeked through the window. Prep tables, cooking stations, back door at the far end. He strolled back to the lobby and out the rear of the hotel to a patio restaurant. Umbrella tables, outside bar, table service. He noted the exit from the kitchen on his right. No surprises. Everything just as it should be.

He rented a golf cart and drove back through the dunes to the derelict cabins. Hernandez and three of the men were already there. One stood guard at the corner of the cabin closest to the golf cart path, a short-barrel Colt M4 assault rifle in his hands. Farther in, Hernandez was opening the boxes of gear on the weedy turf behind the cabin where they'd been stored. The other two men were checking and loading assault rifles and Glock pistols.

Hernandez turned to Raymond, a Kevlar vest in his hands. "The boss splurged on the equipment."

"You know what he says: the best equipment plus the best men equals the best result."

Raymond took off his jacket and his shirt and put on the Kevlar vest over his t-shirt. Then he put his shirt and jacket back on. "How does it look?"

"Can't see it at all. But you'll need to switch to one of these oversize jackets if you're going to hide the M4 on your back." Hernandez glanced at the other men, then whispered, "So what's the job?"

Raymond took a step closer. "Kidnapping."

"Who?" Hernandez asked.

"Smithson's grandson."

Hernandez's eyes lit up. "The boss has got some balls on him."

"He always plays for keeps."

"So everything about this score is by the book until after the ransom."

"Unfortunately. Makes it tougher for us, but so it goes. See you on the other side."

. . .

O'BRIAN WALKED AROUND behind the hotel reception counter and stood next to Lulu while she finished helping a group of middle-aged women check in for their gal pal weekend. As the last one turned to go, he pushed a piece of paper to her. "Here's the final registration details for the Smithsons. I'll take the keycards."

"Yes, sir," she said. "They're right here. Twelfth floor, west wing."

"All of the rooms?"

"Yes, sir. Complete privacy as you requested."

"Thank you, Lulu."

As he walked away, she smiled, held up a finger at the next couple in line, and then picked up the desk phone and input Raymond's cell number.

"Yeah?"

"They're all checked in. It's a definite go."

"Good luck."

AT NOON, JB, Lulu, Max, and Kelly Jo were gathering for lunch at a round table on the employees' patio by the landscapers' garage. Kelly Jo was doing her best full-on jealous rage, as if Max had just done something new to stir her up. She crashed her tray down in the spot between Max and Lulu, gave him the evil eye, and tore off the wrapper on her sandwich. After the first bite, she said. "God, I picked up the wrong sandwich. I hate egg salad."

"Can I go get you something else, honey?" Max asked.

"Fuck you," she muttered.

Lulu covered her smirk with her napkin.

JB smiled. "Here, have half of this roast beef."

"Why, thank you, JB," Kelly Jo said.

Max shook his head and sighed.

Kelly Jo turned on him. "What have you got to sigh about?"

"Do we have to do this here?"

"Anywhere you're flirting with little bitches. That's where we've got to do this. You think I can't see?"

Max rolled his eyes and held up his hands in surrender.

JB swallowed his bite of sandwich and took a drink of Coke. "You guys all set for two o'clock?"

"Yeah," Max said. "I tucked the pistols in under the stack of sheets on the bottom shelf of the service closet."

"We're not going to need them," Lulu said.

"Better have them and not need them, than need them and not have them."

Kelly Jo muttered, "You're so full of it."

JB stood up from the table. "Okay then, I'll meet you up there. I've got to get back to the shop. Crier's been after me for taking too long at lunch."

"I've got to get back, too," Lulu said.

"Then we'll see you on the twelfth floor," Max said.

They watched Lulu and JB walk back up the hill toward the hotel. Kelly Jo set her half-eaten sandwich on her tray. "Do you think I over-played it?"

"You did fine. It was all they could do to keep from laughing at me. They're going up to the twelfth floor, and they're expecting us to join them. God knows what they're planning, but it doesn't matter because we won't be there."

"We've got all our pieces on the board," she said.

"I hope they're the right pieces. So? Stay or go?"

"We run now, we'll never know if we could have taken the whole score."

"We won't even know what the score was."

"It's worth the risk to stay for the show," she said. "Koenig is going to steal something, and I want to know what it is."

SHORTLY AFTER 1:00 P.M., Max and Kelly Jo were jogging down the switchback behind the landscapers' garages. Max was carrying their go bag, just in case they couldn't go back to the motel. The morning haze had lifted, giving them a view all the way to the mainland. Down below, Anders was waiting in an open motor boat with padded lockers running down each side, a captain's hat pulled down over his eyes.

"Can you get any closer?" Max yelled.

Anders shook his head. "No can do. I'm about to bottom out."

Max and Kelly Jo waded thigh deep out in the water. Anders helped them climb up the stern ladder. Water ran off their pants legs into the bottom of the boat.

"Where's the gear?" Max asked.

"Under the benches."

Max lifted the padded seat on the nearest locker, pulled out a white Kevlar vest, and passed it to Kelly Jo. "It looks more or less like a life jacket."

She put it on. He brought out another one for himself.

"Where to?" Anders asked.

"Move around to where we can watch for any boats headed into the VIP marina. We want to be able to cut them off."

They motored around the island until they had a good view of the mainland and the VIP marina. A windsurfer cut back and forth in the north side of the bay. "How's this?" Anders asked.

Max nodded. "Now we wait. If no one is coming by two twenty, we head into the marina to take whatever they're leaving with."

At 1:30 p.m., at the cabins by the east dock, Raymond had gathered his teams together. "Okay, let's review the plan. Hernandez's crew takes the casino. You collect the guards, drive off the bystanders. You set the charges in the exterior wall next to the hotel lobby to create a diversion for your escape. In the meantime, my team will grab the valuables. We mix in with the civilians and meet back at the safe house in town." He glanced over the group. No one spoke. "Let's do this."

The men checked their assault rifles one last time before they slung them onto their backs, muzzles down, and hid them under their loose jackets. Hernandez whistled. seven of the men drifted over to him, and they started through the dunes to the golf cart path. The remaining three men gathered around Raymond. "You guys ready? Everyone know their part?"

The men nodded.

"Follow me."

They walked off in the opposite direction from Hernandez's crew. Raymond's golf cart was waiting for them beside the path. They drove off up the hill into the woods headed for the patio restaurant behind the hotel.

AT 2:15, JB and Lulu were already up in the service closet on the twelfth floor. They had both of the pistols Max had left there. "I wonder what's keeping Max and Kelly Jo," Lulu said.

"I don't know, and I don't care," JB replied. "Just as long as they show up in time to die. I can't wait to see the look on his face when he realizes just how far we played them."

"She really was pissed off, wasn't she?"

"He must not get out very often."

"Or he's better at covering it up when she doesn't get a selfie."

"You sent her a photo?"

"The boss said to move fast."

"No wonder she was spitting fire," JB said.

"How much time do we have?"

"From two thirty? Thirty minutes to meet Raymond downstairs."

"So we're going to need their help to get to all the safes."

"Meaning?"

"You can't shoot them until we're ready to go."

"That's up to them."

"We should stick together. Just in case things go sideways."

"Really? You think Kelly Jo will partner with you or let Max partner with you? The tricky part will be when we meet at the last safe."

"I'll be the straggler," Lulu said. "They won't expect anything if we don't seem organized."

. . .

OUT IN THE BAY, Max, Kelly Jo, and Anders sat on the boat watching the coast and the VIP marina. A few water skiers zoomed by, a few fishing boats floated in the distance, but there was no yacht coming from the mainland—nothing fast enough or big enough to contain a million dollars in dirty money and a security crew. Max looked at his watch. 2:20 p.m. "Anders, nobody's coming. Take us in to the marina."

AT 2:30 P.M., Hernandez's men were loitering around at the entrance to the casino. They pulled down their ski masks, swung their M4 assault rifles around from their backs, and burst through the heavy glass doors. Three uniformed guards at the security desk reached for their pistols. One of Hernandez's men bashed the nearest guard in the face with the butt of his rifle. "Die here or live," Hernandez said. "It's up to you."

The guards put up their hands. Hernandez's men took their pistols and cuffed their hands behind their backs. A few nearby guests who could see what was happening started moving quietly toward the doors of the casino. Hernandez's men herded the guards together. "To the cashiers' cages," Hernandez said. As they started moving, one of Hernandez's crew fired a burst of automatic fire into the ceiling. "Run!" he yelled.

Guests screamed and stampeded for the doors. "Terrorists!" someone yelled. The security alarm sounded, the ringing echoing off the walls. Hernandez's men hustled the guards back through the casino.

MEANWHILE, Raymond and his team of three were positioned in the hall outside the private dining rooms. As soon as he heard the alarm from the casino, he pulled the fire alarm in the hall. Diners rushed from the dining rooms, confusion on their faces. Raymond spotted the Smithson entourage moving down the hall as a unit—they all looked just like their pictures. The old man, gray-faced and slow, his son, Tim, wire-framed glasses and dad bod, his daughter in-law,

Myrna, gym-toned and tan, O'Brian and Ninovich behind them, and a bodyguard on each side. The grandson, Mikey, a small, dark-haired boy in a black suit, was being moved along by the bodyguard on the left side, a big man who was holding the boy's hand.

Raymond motioned to his men. They pushed into Smithson's group as if they were confused about the location of the exits. One of Raymond's men shot the bodyguard point blank. Before any of Smithson's people could react in the pandemonium, Raymond snatched the boy up onto his shoulder and rushed off down the hall, his men swarming around the boy and him as they pushed through the double doors into the kitchen. Ninovich and the other bodyguard charged after them, guns drawn.

"Diego; Juan." Raymond motioned back toward the doors. Two of the men took cover behind refrigerators to set an ambush. "Come on, Sanchez." The remaining man fell in behind Raymond as he carried Mikey out the back door onto the restaurant patio. It was chaos. Guests were yelling and running in all directions, knocking over chairs and pushing tables into each other. A helicopter was hovering above. Raymond waved at the pilot. Mikey was kicking and pounding Raymond's back.

"Hold him," Raymond said to Sanchez. He dropped Mikey to the ground. Sanchez gripped the boy by his shoulders. Raymond cuffed Mikey's hands behind his back. The helicopter touched down. Sanchez lifted Mikey into the helicopter. As Raymond seat-belted Mikey in, Sanchez hooked a control line to his belt and turned in the door of the helicopter, his M4 rifle at the ready.

"Let's go," Raymond yelled. The helicopter pilot nodded, and they took off.

MAX AND KELLY JO were running up the path from the marina when they saw Raymond burst out of the back of the hotel with another armed man, a boy in a black suit over his shoulder. Alarms shrieked out of the building. Max and Kelly Jo watched as the helicopter set down and Raymond and his accomplice shoved the boy onboard.

Two more gunmen rushed out of the back of the hotel, looked up at the helicopter flying away, and then dropped their rifles in the nearest trashcan before pulling off their jackets and disappearing into the crowd.

"Let's get back to the boat. This is swirling down the toilet," Max said.

They ran back to the marina, mixing in with the terrified guests who were looking for any way to escape. Their boat was bobbing in the water near to the dock. Anders spotted them and motored up. They climbed on board.

A fat man wearing plaid shorts, his combover hanging down in his eyes, held up his wallet. "Take me with you. I can pay!"

Max shook his head. Anders started to back the boat away from the dock. The man grabbed for the side railing. Max showed him his pistol. "Let go."

The fat man threw his hands up. His wallet flipped into the air and plopped down into the water. Max turned to Anders. "Let's get out of here. We're on the backup plan."

THE SMITHSON FAMILY was huddled together in the hallway. Myrna Smithson, Mikey's mother, was on her knees, her face in her hands, sobbing. Her husband, Tim, knelt beside her, rubbing her back, whispering. The other bodyguard knelt over the one who'd been shot, keeping pressure on the wound, while the hotel nurse practitioner rummaged in her medical bag. Jeffrey Smithson stood by the wall, huddled with his lieutenants, talking in a low voice. "What's being done?"

"Everything is still a mess. We know that two of those guys took Mikey in a helicopter. The other two are still here somewhere. There's a robbery crew trapped in the casino. The casino security team has the casino and the outside covered, so we're searching the building before the cops get here," O'Brian replied. "We've blocked the ferry and the marina. Nobody's leaving this island without our say-so."

"My guys are watching the ferry dock in town," Ninovich said. "We'll catch the guys who were left behind. We're going to know everything they know."

"I'm going to kill those guys. I'm going to kill all of them," Smithson said.

"They won't hurt Mikey," O'Brian said.

"Hurt him? They hurt him, and I'll wipe out every one of their families. Grandmas, grandpas, aunts, uncles, everyone."

Smithson glanced at his son and daughter in-law. There was nothing he could do for them. He stepped over to the nurse practitioner. "How's Allen?"

"We need the ambulance as soon as possible," she said.

He turned to O'Brian.

"Ambulances are on the ferry right now."

BY 2:50 P.M., the private security assault team had turned off the alarms and taken control of the entrance and emergency exits to the casino. Inside, the casino was strangely quiet except for the odd slot machine noise and the whir of the air-conditioning system. The security guards and the cashiers were all sitting on the floor, their hands and ankles zip-tied. Five of Hernandez's men stood over them, talking in Spanish. Hernandez got out his burner phone to call Raymond. No answer. What did he expect? No matter how the kidnapping went, they were on their own. He walked over to the corner of the room nearest the hotel lobby. His other two men had just finished setting explosives against the wall. "All ready?"

"Say when," the taller one replied.

Hernandez whistled back to the others, who started across the room. Then Hernandez and the demolition team ran back behind a row of slot machines. The explosion blew a gaping hole into the hotel lobby. The sprinkler system came on. Hernandez and his crew rushed through the hole into the lobby and out through the exit to the patio restaurant, ditching their jackets and weapons as they ran. Once outside, they scattered, mixing in with the panicked guests who were still wandering the property, as the assault team hurried onto the patio looking for them.

UPSTAIRS IN THE HOTEL, two of Smithson's men, burly guys in shapeless suits, got off the elevator on the twelfth floor. As they moved down the hall, JB and Lulu came out of one of the suites, each carrying a small gray duffel.

The men pulled their pistols. "Stop," the smaller one said.

"Whoa," JB said, holding up his hands, "we're hotel employees."

"What are you doing up here?"

"Something kicked off the fire alarm, so we're checking the electrical systems in the rooms."

He pointed at Lulu. "She's not in maintenance."

"We're short on staff with all the commotion."

"Let me see the bags."

The taller man started toward JB. He threw his duffel at him and turned to run. The shorter one fired his gun. JB stumbled and fell. Lulu huddled against the wall, whimpering, her hands in front of her face.

"You shot me." JB held his lower leg. Blood leaked between his fingers.

"Doesn't look too bad," the shorter one said. He glanced at his associate. "The bag."

The taller one unzipped the duffel. "Jewelry and cash." Lulu's duffel lay at her feet. He snatched it up and looked inside. "More of the same."

Lulu looked from the taller to the shorter one. "He made me do it. It was all his idea."

The shorter one shook his head. "Don't care."

She gestured at JB. "He threatened me, said he'd hurt me if I didn't help him. I don't know anything about all this."

"You hold on to that story," the shorter one said. "I'm sure the boss is going to love it."

"Just let me go. I'll make it worth your while."

"You're going to make it worth my while anyway." He got out his phone. "We found two of them."

Hernandez jogged down the golf-cart path on the east side of the island, heading back to the broken-down dock. His boat should be waiting there. What he hadn't told Raymond was that the key to working with Koenig on his high-risk, high-reward jobs was to always have your own getaway plan. Did Koenig's people always end up dead or in jail by design or just through bad luck? He hadn't ever really though much about it. He'd always done well working with Koenig, and you could be sure that after a job was over, there was never any blowback.

He ran between the dunes and out onto the pea gravel. There it was. The little motorboat he'd rented yesterday. His cousin waved to him from the cockpit. He slipped his hand into his pocket and gripped the butt of his pistol, just in case there was someone else hidden on the boat. If Raymond had the kid, the money was as good as theirs. Nothing was going to keep him from making it to the safe house.

The helicopter flew over the bay south to Lover's Point. Mikey was whimpering, holding his jaw tight to keep from blubbering. Raymond studied him, thinking about his life, his choices, what he might be capable of if he thought his situation was hopeless. Sure, he was a twelve-year-old rich kid, used to being pampered, but that didn't mean he should be underestimated. He might try to escape, try to drop a clue, try to hurt himself. None of those were acceptable.

At Lover's Point, the helicopter set down in a field just behind the parking lot. "Kid," Raymond said, "you've got nothing to worry about. This is just business. Your gramps is going to pay. By Monday afternoon, you'll be home. You understand me?"

Mikey wouldn't look at his face.

"We don't want to hurt you. You do what you're told, you'll be as comfortable as we can make you. Food, TV, games, the works."

Mikey nodded.

"But right now, I need to blindfold you and put these noise-cancelling headphones on you. It's for your own protection."

He blindfolded Mikey and put the headset on him. He turned to Sanchez. "Go get the car."

Sanchez trotted over to the parking lot, his assault rifle hidden under his jacket, and climbed into a Ford Transit with tinted windows. Raymond led Mikey across the field. When they got to the parking lot, the helicopter took off. He got into the back seat of the Transit with Mikey and buckled him in, and then patted the back of the front seat. "Nice and easy," he said to Sanchez. "We're home free now."

6

THE COPS

Detective Gower with the organized crime taskforce got off the ferry and started up the walkway to the casino hotel. He was a blocky man with a gray crewcut and a perpetual scowl. A uniformed officer glanced at him, saw the badge hanging from his sportscoat breast pocket, and nodded. Gower nodded back. Trash and pieces of clothing were scattered over the grounds, tables and chairs near the fast-food kiosks were all askew, groups of people were meandering aimlessly or talking in small groups. Four uniformed officers stood at the ferry dock checking IDs and taking down information from a long line of guests waiting to leave the island. They were like passengers waiting in a TSA line at the airport on a holiday weekend. Indignant, resigned, relieved. So much for the weekend getaway.

To his left, paramedics were set up under the picnic shelter attending those injured in the initial crush. The front of the casino hotel was marked off by police tape and temporary barriers, while crime scene markers were scattered over the steps by the doorway. He rubbed his hand over his head. An attempted casino robbery. Jeffrey Smithson's grandson kidnapped. Who would be stupid enough to kidnap Michael Smithson? Up ahead he saw his partner, Jamil Johnson, waiting at the hotel entrance. He looked completely at ease. A skinny black guy with his hands in the pockets of his tan suit. Gower still didn't know how Johnson was getting away with the cornrows at his age. "How did you get here so fast?"

"Why did it take you so long?"

"I was out on Putnam golf course."

"Traffic must have been a bitch."

"All the way across town." He squinted to see into the interior. "What have we got?"

Johnson pulled a notepad from his pocket. "Looks like twelve perpetrators, two teams. Eight guys hit the casino. Four guys went for the kid. Two casino robbers shot dead by the private rapid response. Robbers blasted through the wall of the casino to escape into the hotel. One of Smithson's guys shot bad during the kidnapping."

"Any surveillance footage?"

"Up the wazoo. Casino, hotel registration, the grounds. It's going to take some time to go through it all. We're getting complete cooperation."

"Who's in charge?"

"Harold O'Brian."

"Smithson's guy?"

"He's passed muster with the gaming commission."

"Is the building clear?"

"We're still searching the upper floors of the hotel."

"Grounds are going to be a pain in the ass, what with the woods and the marina."

"Yeah, this is one hell of a crime scene. We've got the marina locked down, but there's too much rough terrain."

Gower noticed two young men filming them with their smartphones and called over to a nearby uniformed officer. "Richards. Tell those tourists to put their phones away. Get their info and move them along." He turned back to Johnson. "What were the Smithsons doing here?"

"It's his birthday."

"His birthday? So it was a family gathering?"

"Son, daughter in-law, grandson, plus O'Brian and Ninovich and four soldiers that we know of."

"O'Brian is mixing with them out in the open?"

"His shtick is that he's just offering the resort's support to an important guest during this trying time."

"Where are they?"

"Private dining room."

"Let's get this over with."

They walked up through the heavy dust and the concrete rubble in the hotel lobby and turned into the restaurant. In the main dining room, one server was vacuuming while others were already cleaning up the tables, setting new tablecloths, and resetting the chairs. To the right, two men the size of football linemen stood at the door to the farthest private dining room. They stepped aside for Gower and Johnson. Smithson—black suit, white shirt, no tie—was sitting by himself at the head of a long table, half-filled glasses and unfinished plates of food marking the empty places. O'Brian and Ninovich were hovering around like they were waiting for orders. The detectives ignored them.

"Mr. Smithson, I'm Detective Gower, and this is Detective Johnson."

"I know who you are. You're with organized crime."

"And we know who you are. But make no mistake, we're going to do everything we can to get your grandson back. May we sit?"

He nodded.

"Where's your son and your daughter in-law?"

"They went up to their room. She's hysterical. He's called their doctor."

"Can you tell us how it happened?"

"We were eating. Fire alarm went off. They were waiting in the hall. They shot Allen. Grabbed Mikey. Two of my guys went after them, but they got away."

"Your people are armed? I thought guests weren't allowed to carry guns here."

"There're special rules for VIPs. Professional bodyguards."

"So everyone has a permit?"

"Yes."

"Mr. Smithson, can you point us in the right direction? Does this kidnapping have anything to do with your business?"

"That's crazy. It's got nothing to do with us. They took my grandson. You should be focusing on that."

"There're teams of people working this crime scene. And there're surveillance cameras all over this island. We're going to find out who did this. If they're in the system, we're going to know who they are," Gower said. "In the meantime, you're going to get a ransom demand. It's going to come fast. When the kidnappers call you, you need to call us. We'll get your grandson back."

"You really think you can get him back safe?"

"We're trained for this, Mr. Smithson. We'll get him back. And don't say anything to the media," Gower continued. "We're going to keep the kidnapping completely quiet."

"One other thing," Johnson added. "We're going to need information on all of your people who are on the island."

"None of my people had anything to do with this," Smithson said.

"Everybody on the island has to be cleared."

Gower and Johnson stood up. "Here's my card," Gower said. "If you remember anything else, or if the kidnappers get in touch, that's my cell number. Day or night."

"Okay," Smithson said.

Gower and Johnson walked back through the restaurant and out past the wreckage in the lobby. "He's not going to call us," Johnson said.

"No, he's not. He's going to try to take care of this himself."

"I feel sorry for the kid and his parents," Johnson said. "They aren't in the business."

"Yeah, it's a shitty deal for them, but it's a great opportunity for us," Gower replied. "Let's try to get them all under surveillance. We can piggyback on whatever they do to get the kid back, and maybe we'll catch them up in a crime along the way."

"You know they're going to get a copy of the island surveillance footage."

"Yeah, usually that would piss me off. But in this case, kidnapping a kid, if they can get him back without killing any innocents, I'll call it a win."

BACK IN THE private dining room, Ninovich and O'Brian had sat down at the table. Smithson was stirring sugar into his coffee. "Who are they kidding? Putting them in the loop is the quickest way to get Mikey killed." He rapped his teaspoon on the table. "What have you got so far?"

"My guys scooped up three of them trying to get off the ferry in town," Ninovich said.

"Good. Where did you take them?"

"Fifth Street warehouse."

"And we've got the two we found on the twelfth floor," O'Brian said.

"Grifters?"

"They were robbing the hotel rooms. They had the room safe master keycode."

"That sounds like something. Get them off the island as soon as possible. Take them to the warehouse with the other three. We're going to find out everything they know."

"Yes, sir."

Smithson looked at each of his lieutenants in turn. "Keep digging. I'm going to check on my family. Meet me at the office in two hours."

ANDERS EASED the motorboat up to the public docks at Connor's Cove State Park. Max and Kelly Jo had put their Kevlar vests, weapons, and go bag into two duffels. They'd passed several fishing boats on the way in, their occupants on deck working their fishing rods. A dozen cars were parked in the gravel lot. Anders handed Max a set of keys and a scrap of paper with an address on it. He pointed to a Sentra at the far end of the lot. "The gray one. It should be safe for a couple of days. The house is good for a week. The storage locker is paid up for the month. I'll get rid of this boat and be in touch."

Max nodded.

"Thanks," Kelly Jo said.

"Hell of a gamble, but I guess we're done," Anders said.

"No," Max replied. "We're not done yet. You're still in for a fifth. It's just going to take longer to get it."

Max and Kelly Jo carried their gear across the lot to the Sentra and loaded it into the trunk. Kelly Jo got into the driver's seat. Full tank of gas. She drove out of the parking lot, headed toward Bathsheba City. Max got out Koenig's phone and called him. He got a no-service recording. He pulled the chip from the phone and threw the chip and the phone out the window. "Koenig sure planned this right."

"We escaped."

"Who was that kid?"

"The one in the confirmation suit? No idea."

"We need to find out what's going on."

He took out his own phone, called Zeb, and filled him in. "Give me a call when you know something."

"I'll see what I can do."

They drove into a neighborhood of small, single-story houses near a school that had been closed down. On Tulip Street, Kelly Jo turned up the driveway of a ranch-style house next to a two-story house with a FOR SALE sign in the yard and pulled into the attached garage. The house was furnished. The freezer was full of pizza and TV dinners. The refrigerator had beer, soft drinks and milk. There was bread and breakfast cereal in the cabinets. "Looks like we could stay here a while," Kelly Jo said.

"We're going to keep our heads down for a few days."

"We'll need to pick up some clothes."

"Yeah. Hope you weren't attached to anything we left at the motel."

. . .

AT GALAXY YACHT SALES, Smithson and his lieutenants sat around the desk in Smithson's office. "Kidnappers spoke Spanish to each other," Smithson said. "So it could be Rey's drug crew making a move."

"That's not their style," Ninovich said. "They've never gone after families."

"But what about the Salvadorans?" O'Brian asked. "They'll do anything."

Ninovich worried a gum wrapper between his fingers. "We won't know who they are until they make their demands."

"But you're supposed to know what the competition is up to," Smithson said. "I want you out on the streets shaking down anyone who might know anything."

He turned to O'Brian. "And you were in charge of our security."

"We're going to look hard at everyone. Heads are going to roll."

"They were moving around the island like they owned the place."

"Don't worry, sir. If anyone's dirty, we'll find them."

"If anyone's dirty? Two of your employees were robbing our rooms. You better get your house in order. Somebody on the island sold us out, helped kidnap my grandson. And now the place is crawling with cops. God knows what they'll find while they're investigating."

"They won't find anything. Period. The money is completely safe. As soon as the cops are out of the way, we're back in business."

Smithson turned to Ninovich. "You're running security at the warehouse."

"My people are already set up," O'Brian said.

"Yeah, and your people got screwed on your home turf, so all your people are suspect." Smithson got out his inhaler, shook it, and sucked a puff into his lungs. "From here on out, there's going to be no more mistakes. Ninovich's people are in the clear. That means he's walking point."

"We'll get Mikey back," Ninovich said. "We'll find out who did this. They're all dead. Every last one of them."

Smithson turned to O'Brian. "Have you started questioning the ones we rounded up?"

He nodded.

"Have they told us anything yet?"

"Not yet."

Ninovich tossed the gum wrapper into the trash can. "I've got a couple of guys who will make them talk."

"Don't accidently kill them. We need to know everything they know before they die." Smithson drummed his fingers on the table as he looked from Ninovich to O'Brian. "Both of you put out feelers. We'll pay for Mikey. As soon as he's safe, we'll start hunting these assholes. They'll never enjoy a penny of that money. Now get out of here and do your jobs."

O'Brian and Ninovich walked through the sales office and out into the parking lot. "This was supposed to be our day," O'Brian said.

"So much for that," Ninovich replied.

"Anything you need, you just let me know."

"Thanks," Ninovich said. "You got your work cut out for you."

"I'll be back in business inside the week."

"That's great news. I hate to sit on too big a pile of cash. Good luck getting your people sorted." Ninovich walked off to his Mercedes Benz.

O'Brian climbed into his BMW. He needed to prove to Smithson that he still deserved his job. He called his IT manager. "Martin. You need to get into the office. JB Turner, maintenance tech, and Lulu Osmond, front desk. Run face recognition on the surveillance footage going back a month. I want to know where they went and who they were with on the island. Any patterns that might be suspicious. I need this info as soon as possible."

"Yes, sir."

HERNANDEZ DROVE into the garage of the Ridgeway safehouse and parked next to the Ford Transit. As he was getting out of the car, the door to the kitchen opened. Sanchez stood there holding an M-4 rifle. "*Hola.*"

Sanchez nodded.

"Did you get the kid?"

Another nod.

"Who's here?"

"Just Raymond."

They walked through the kitchen to the living room. The TV was on a local news channel. Raymond came up the stairs from the basement. "You made it," Raymond said.

"It was a good plan."

"Sanchez, go downstairs and keep an eye on the kid."

Raymond waited for Sanchez to disappear down the stairs before he continued. "How did you get off the island?"

"I made my own arrangements."

"Smart move."

"How many guys got away?"

"We don't know yet." Raymond nodded toward the TV, which showed the police checkpoint at the ferry dock from two hours earlier. "They should start trickling in. Everyone should be here before midnight."

"Everyone alive. Where's Koenig?" Hernandez asked.

"He'll be here tomorrow."

"And that's when he'll share the details?"

"As many as he has to."

"From here on out, every step of the way becomes more dangerous," Hernandez said.

"Until we have the money."

"Until we've dealt with Koenig. He's not just going to let us walk away with the score."

"One step at a time, my friend, one step at a time," Raymond said. "First we have to get rid of the kid and get the cash. Then we'll deal with Koenig."

"How's that?"

"We're the best guys to do the swap. Koenig has got to send us. We hand off the kid, we get the money. If nothing goes wrong, we run with the cash. It's the best opportunity we're going to get. If Koenig gets his hands on the money, taking it'll be ten times more difficult."

"If we stiff him, he'll be hot after us."

"He'll be too late."

7

WHEELING AND DEALING

The next morning, Max and Kelly Jo sat in the living room of the Tulip Street house drinking coffee and keeping an eye on the street. The casino heist was on all the morning news shows and the internet, but there was no news about a kidnapping. "Should we run?" Kelly Jo asked.

"Anders dropped us in a nice spot. We've got everything we need. Every corner that the cops aren't watching, one of Smithson's people is. I vote we stay, at least for now."

"Eventually the cops are going to find us on the surveillance footage."

"But we're not doing anything illegal on the footage, right? So we'll be low priority for facial recognition."

"But when we don't show up for work—"

"News story said they won't be open until next week."

"Okay, so we've got a few days. We still need to work on our exit strategy."

"I agree. Our problem now is that we don't know what we don't know. Who was the kid they took? What's he worth? Who's going to be pissed? But we're in pretty good shape. We've got some money and new IDs in our PO box. We'll need a fresh car, but that's no big deal. Do you want some more coffee?"

She passed him her cup. He went into the kitchen, filled their cups, and brought them back.

"Thanks," she said.

He sat back down. "Koenig has got to trade the kid."

"But we don't know where Koenig is or when that's going to happen."

"And we can't be out and about because of the cops and Smithson's crew."

"Maybe Zeb will know something," Kelly Jo said.

"Maybe."

LATER, after lunch, while Max was reading the newsfeed on his phone, looking for any new information about the casino heist, Zeb called. "It's worse than you can imagine. That kid is Smithson's grandson. You need to tie off any loose ends and get gone."

"Thanks, Zeb."

Kelly Jo was loading the dishwasher when Max told her. "So that was the deal all along," she said. "There was no money delivery this weekend. We were just part of the diversion."

"He probably wasn't planning to retire at all."

She wiped her hands on a dishtowel. "What do you think the ask is?"

"One million, five million, it doesn't matter. Messing with that kid, that's Russian roulette with all the chambers loaded. As soon as Smithson has the kid back, and figures out who did it, it's pliers and blowtorch. And if the kid's got a scratch on him..."

"Glad I don't have anything to pack. We running for the airport?"

"Our IDs are probably blown. The new ones are downtown in the Mail-N-More PO box. So let's just sit tight. Wait for dark. It's been almost twenty-four hours. Smithson has gotten a call, or he's going to get a call. All he has to do is snap his fingers to pull the money together, so this is going to happen fast."

"And while Smithson's people are focused on the kid, we slip out of here."

"Once it's dark, if nothing's happened, we get out of town, switch cars and run like hell."

MIDAFTERNOON, the Smithsons were gathered at the family compound on Rocky Shore Drive. Armed guards manned the gates and walked the perimeter on the shore side of the property. Smithson and his son, Tim, sat in the family room of the mansion. The football game was on the TV, but no one was watching it. "I haven't seen Myrna," Smithson said. "Is she doing any better?"

Tim sighed. "She can't seem to get out of bed. I think the medicine is helping, though."

"We'll get Mikey back. That's the medicine she needs. You wait and see, everything is going to work out."

The landline rang. Smithson picked it up. "Mr. Smithson, two million in dirty money. Two bags. One million in each bag. Three o'clock tomorrow. You and two of your guys. The boy's parents can come if they like. We'll call with the address at two o'clock."

"I want to speak to Mikey."

"No can do. No one is going to hurt the kid. He's not in the game. This is business. Bring the money to the spot. Do what you're told. We'll trade the kid straight up. You want the kid; we want the money." The line went dead.

"Was it them?" Tim asked.

"We're getting Mikey back tomorrow."

"I'm coming with you."

"We'll see."

"I'm coming."

Smithson patted Tim's shoulder. "Think this through. We won't be pulling our punches."

"Mikey's going to be there. I'm his dad. I'm going to be there."

"Okay. I understand. Just do yourself a favor. Don't ask any questions. Don't see anything you don't need to see."

"I know, Pop."

"I don't think you do know, Timmy. It all goes perfect, you may end up having to give a statement or having to testify under oath. It goes bad, you might end up shot or at the hospital. Are you ready for that?"

"I'm coming, Pop. I don't care about any of that. I'll do whatever I have to do to protect Mikey."

"Okay, then. But I'm not giving you a gun."

"I don't want a gun."

Smithson hugged his son. "Let me make the arrangements."

He walked out onto the patio and got out his cell phone. "O'Brian, I need two million in old bills, ASAP. Deliver it to Ninovich today." He ended that call and called Ninovich. "We're on for tomorrow at three o'clock."

"Where?"

"They'll tell us at two. Me, Tim, you, and one of your guys. O'Brian's people will deliver the money to you today. Two million. Count it. You need to be ready to go. No mistakes."

"You and Tim don't need to be there. Mikey knows me."

"We're going to be there."

"Okay, I'll take care of all the details. I'll be at Rocky Shore Drive at two."

The line was quiet.

"Mr. Smithson?" Ninovich asked.

"Do you know who did this yet?"

"We're making progress. A guy who works for us told us about a guy who may be helpful. We're tracking him down."

"What about the idiots we scooped up?"

"They don't know anything."

"You sure?"

"They'd tell us if they knew. They always do."

"Call me as soon as you know anything." Smithson ended the call.

IN THE BASEMENT of the Ridgeway safehouse, Raymond watched

Mikey in the special room through the two-way mirror. A TV with a game console stood against one wall. The toilet and sink were in the far corner. A McDonald's bag sat on a shelf in front of a small sliding door. But Mikey wasn't eating or playing a game. He just sat on the sofa fidgeting.

Raymond spoke over the speaker. "Relax, kid. No one in your family was hurt. You don't have to believe me. Turn on the TV and look at the news."

Mikey glanced around until he found the speaker the voice was coming from. "Let me out of here."

"I know you're uncomfortable, but no one is going to hurt you. You're too valuable. Your gramps will pay, and you'll be back with your family tomorrow. So relax, eat, sleep. Tomorrow will be here before you know it."

Raymond turned to Hernandez. "We need to make sure someone is down here watching this kid all the time. Nothing happens to him."

"He can't get out."

"What if he tries to hurt himself? Somebody watches him all the time."

Raymond went up the stairs. Koenig was sitting in the dining room, working at his laptop computer, double-checking the routes and details for the exchange. "How is he?"

"Quiet. He hasn't eaten anything."

"Get a pint of ice cream out of the freezer. The one with the chocolate swirls. I bet he'll eat some of that."

"Good idea."

"There's nothing to worry about, Raymond. The kid's not going to get hurt. Before the end of the month, he'll be bragging to his friends about how tough he was."

Raymond nodded toward the computer. "Everything check out?"

"We're set. The exchange site, the next safe house, all the details in between have the usual redundancies."

"We lost two guys on the island. Plus Lulu and JB. And three guys are missing."

"It was to be expected. None of them can talk because they don't know anything. We still have five guys, as well as you and Hernandez, moving forward. Tomorrow we make the exchange. Then everything gets easier."

"I'll take Hernandez to make the exchange. The kid trusts me, and Hernandez is our best guy."

Koenig shook his head. "That's why Hernandez has to stay with me. Anything goes sideways, I might need him. You take Sanchez. The kid's already seen him."

AFTER DINNER, Max was sitting on the sofa in the living room, flipping through the channels on the TV, looking for any updated information on what the media was calling the Solomon Island robbery, when his phone rang. It was Anders.

"Talk."

"I'm sorry, man. But I work for Ninovich all the time. I told him you didn't have anything to do with the kidnap—"

Max sprang to his feet and crammed his phone into his pocket. He yelled down the hall. "Run!"

Kelly Jo sprinted out of the bedroom, pulling on her jacket as she headed toward the door to the garage. Max was right behind her. She pressed the garage door opener. He dove into the driver's seat of the Sentra and jammed the shifter into reverse. She was slamming her door as the car raced backward down the driveway. The tires squealed as Max turned the wheel and stomped on the brakes. He shoved the shifter into Drive. They left the garage door open. He turned right at the first intersection, and then left, taking the shortest route to the boulevard and the freeway. As he sped along, he filled her in.

"Damn it," Kelly Jo said. "I never thought Anders would sell us out."

"He lives here. At least he gave us the heads-up."

He heard the short bleat of a police siren and saw blue lights in his rearview mirror. He flipped on his turn signal and pulled over. The police cruiser pulled in behind him. He kept his hands on the steering wheel. A woman officer, her hand on the butt of her holstered pistol, came up to his window. He lowered it.

"License and registration, please."

"My license is in my back pocket."

She nodded. He dug out his wallet and got out his driver's license.

He glanced at Kelly Jo. "Honey, could you get the registration from the glove box?"

She found it among the pens, scraps of trash, and loose change and passed it to him. He handed it to the officer.

The officer looked over the license and the registration. "This isn't your car."

"Borrowed."

"Uh-huh. Turn the car off."

He turned the key. The officer went back to her cruiser with his license and the Sentra's registration.

"Will the car hold up?" Kelly Jo asked.

"Anders said two days."

"Not really trusting Anders right now."

"He didn't know he was screwed when he chose the car."

"I'd just hate to kill this cop."

"I know. It would be a lot of extra trouble."

A utility van screeched in at an angle in front of them. Two bruisers jumped out of the front wearing garage coveralls and carrying shotguns. Max and Kelly Jo looked back at the police car. The officer was walking toward them with her pistol drawn. The bruisers opened the doors to the Sentra and pulled Max and Kelly Jo out. "Don't do anything stupid," the one who had Max said. "We can't kill you, but we can fuck you up so you'll wish you were dead."

They pushed Max and Kelly Jo onto the hood of the Sentra and patted them down, taking their pistols and their smartphones before they zip-tied their hands behind their backs.

The one behind Kelly Jo nodded toward the officer. "The boss says he owes you one."

The officer holstered her gun. "You guys taking care of the car?"

"Don't worry about it."

The police officer got back in her cruiser. The two men shoved them into the back of the van. "Sit down."

They sat on the floor. There were no windows in the back of the van and no door handle on the inside of the back door or the side door. Kelly Jo looked at Max. He mouthed the word *Wait*.

After forty minutes of potholed streets and sharp turns, they pulled to a stop. The two bruisers opened the back. "Get out."

They were in a large warehouse. The men led them to a storeroom, unlocked the door, and pushed them inside. The bolt in the door grated home. Max felt along the wall and found a light switch. One bulb burned overhead. The storeroom was ten feet by ten feet, with built-in shelves all along both sides. Two men lay dead at the back of the space. Their legs splayed out at odd angles. Their clothes were tatters. Their faces were unrecognizable masses of bruises and cigarette burns.

"Fuck me," Max said.

They heard screaming from somewhere close by, punctuated by short, intermittent bursts of garbled pleading.

Kelly Jo slipped and banged into the wall. Max stepped up against her to keep her from falling. "You okay?"

"Yeah."

"I know you've had some bad luck in tight places."

"That's an understatement."

"We're not dying here. Right now, Koenig is laughing at us. But we're going to find him. We're going to kill him, and we're going to steal his score. That's what we do."

She took a deep breath and steadied herself. "I'll be okay."

"You sure?"

"Yeah, it was just a physical reaction; my mind's in the game."

He kissed her cheek before he stepped away from her.

"Who do you think they are?"

"Got to be two of Koenig's guys. Let's see what we can do."

He looked along the metal shelves until he found a sharp edge and then ran the zip tie binding his wrists over it until it snapped. "That's the spot."

While Kelly Jo did the same, he got down on his hands and knees and methodically went through the dead men's pockets. Nothing but lint. Then he looked over every inch of the walls. No vents, no repairs, no place that could possibly be forced open. He sat down beside her.

"I could have told you," she said.

"Had to try."

After a while, the door opened. It was the two bruisers who had brought them there. They were carrying a dead man between them. They pitched the body into the room. It landed on the others with a sickening thud. "You been enjoying the company of your friends?" one of them asked.

"Not our friends," Max said.

"Come out of there."

When they stood up, the men noticed that their hands were free. "You've been busy," the other one said.

"Not looking for trouble. Just passing the time."

They pushed them along, guiding them across the open part of the warehouse to a large garage set up for vehicle repair. JB and Lulu, naked and unconscious, dangled from chains run through overhead pulleys, their toes barely touching the floor. A rolling tool bench with knives, pliers, and hammers laid out on its top was positioned beside them. Two folding chairs had been set out facing them. "Have a seat," one of the men said.

They heard a toilet flush. Another man, shorter and beefier, bald on top, came around from behind them. "How are you?"

"I guessing you're Ninovich," Max said.

He smiled and nodded. "Anders is a good man. A company man. He would never screw us over. You two, on the other hand—you were planning to steal from us."

"Not you. We're not that stupid. We were stealing from the guy who's stealing from you."

"And why would you do that?"

"Because that's what we do."

"Running the inside crew, seducing the assistant manager, kidnapping the boss's grandson."

"We didn't have anything to do with the kidnapping."

He nodded toward JB and Lulu. "That's what they said. How do you think that's working out for them?"

"Kidnapping the kid was a gutless move. Ask Anders. That's not the way we work. We don't mess with civilians. Ever. Period."

"Maybe I'll let my boys play with your girl awhile. See if your story changes."

"You're going to do whatever you're going to do, but our story won't change. You want the kid back?"

"We're going to get the kid back."

"What about the guy who planned this thing?"

"Going to kill him."

"You won't even find him. He's a ghost. He's two steps ahead of you, leaving pawns on the table to slow you down. That's what the three casino robbers were. That's what those two are."

"That's what you are."

"You're right. That's my point. Nobody you see is going to be that guy."

"But you know who he is."

"I do. I know who he is and how he works. So I could help you find him. Nobody else can do that."

"So you can kill him and keep our money?"

Max shrugged. "How bad do you want him dead? How bad do you want the complete gratitude of your boss?"

"What's his name?"

"Right now? Right this minute? His name is Koenig. As soon as he has the ransom, he'll disappear and his name will be something else. All you'll catch is more like you already got. Pawns who know nothing useful."

Ninovich took his phone from the pocket of his coveralls and walked away. They could hear him talking, but they couldn't make out what he was saying. When he returned, he turned to his men. "Give them their gear."

One of the bruisers walked away. Max and Kelly Jo sat there, their eyes focused on Ninovich, waiting to hear the rest of it.

"You're going to find this Koenig. You're going to deliver him to me. If you try to run, we'll hunt you down. I'll make it my fulltime job. And after we catch you, you'll wish we had given you the same treatment as your friends here."

"You're getting the kid back?"

"It's already set."

"We need to be at the exchange."

"Why's that?"

"Quickest way to Koenig is to track the money."

"What makes you think we won't be doing that?"

"You won't be able to keep up. I told you, I know him. I know how he works."

"Okay," Ninovich said. "Be ready to go at two o'clock tomorrow. I've got your number."

"Can you get one of those GPS dart guns?"

"There's no flies on you, is there? Yeah, I can get one."

"We'll be waiting for your call."

The bruiser came back, carrying their phones and their guns. "Your car is out front."

They walked out of the security door next to the oversize garage door at the front of the warehouse. It was dark outside. At the corner, under the streetlight, the sign read *Fifth Street*. The Sentra was parked at the curb with the keys in it. Max slid into the driver's seat. Neither of them spoke until they were two blocks away.

"That was a squeaker," Kelly Jo said.

"I'm a closer." Max held up one hand. It was trembling. "Of course, we were lucky in the order. They'd already killed enough people to know that I was right."

"But you still had to sell it."

"You think we should run?"

"Are you kidding?" she asked. "I want Koenig dead as much as you do. We're going to take his money—"

"Skim his money. Most of it will have to go back."

"Skim his money and kill him. And Raymond too. In the beginning I thought that you were being a little obsessive, but now I know why you call Koenig the snake in the Garden of Eden. I still don't know why he would think this was a winning hand."

"With all the collateral damage?"

"Yeah."

"It's the way he always works. You've got to admit his plan was a thing of beauty."

"Baby, it's a thing of beauty if it's happening to someone else."

"True."

"And the kid was off limits."

"Also true. But it makes Smithson crazy. Easier to outsmart."

"So it's back to the house?"

"Might as well. They're probably following us, and we don't want to spook them. We've got to wait for a call. That's as good a place as any."

BACK AT THE WAREHOUSE, two of Ninovich's men loaded the last body from the storeroom off a wheeled cart and into the back of the utility van. Another man was power-washing the storeroom, starting with the ceiling and working his way down the walls. Ninovich stood in the vehicle repair garage, talking on the phone. "Karen, are you tailing them?"

"I put a transmitter on the car. I'm about half a block back."

"Don't lose them. I've called in Sally and Rita. As soon as they get in touch with you, you're done for the day."

He ended the call. One of the men pushed the empty cart into the garage. "Yeah, Chucky?"

"We're ready for these two."

Ninovich operated the pulley control. JB and Lulu lowered into a pile on the floor. Chucky pushed the cart up next to the bodies. "Say, Ninovich, you think the grifters know we had the storeroom bugged?"

"Don't know." He turned away from the garage and speed-dialed Smithson. "It's going just like you wanted."

"You sure?"

"I've put our best trackers on them. Tomorrow we'll get Mikey back, we'll let the grifters find Koenig, and when they've got our guy, we'll kill them all."

"We're not going to have any mistakes."

"Short leash. If they turn out to be trouble, we'll put them in the landfill."

"You get this done, I'm not going to forget you came through."

Smithson ended the call. Ninovich made another call. "Mario? I'm going to need that armored Volvo SUV tomorrow."

"The XC90?"

"Yeah. You're driving."

"Will do."

"And Mario, find me a GPS dart gun."

"I'll have to go to the cops."

"Just do it."

Ninovich put his phone away. So far, so good. Get the kid back. Clear up the mess. He was one step closer to becoming the heir apparent.

SERGEANT PARK, a Korean American with a midwestern accent, sat in a Chevy on Fifth Street across from the warehouse. He'd followed Ninovich here from Galaxy Yacht Sales. The Diet Coke he'd drunk had been a mistake. He was awake all right, but now he needed to pee. He had almost convinced himself to make a quick trip behind the dumpster in the alley behind him when he saw a gray Sentra pull up to the front door of the warehouse. A big guy in coveralls got out. Park picked up his camera. He looked at the license plate through the viewfinder, but the plate was too far into the shadow for him to make out the numbers. A few minutes later, a man and a woman came out of the warehouse. Park took their picture while they were still under the entry light shining down in front of the doors. They got in the Sentra and drove away.

A half hour later, the garage door opened and a utility van drove out. Park managed to photograph its license plate. There was something odd about the van. Was the back end riding low? Was it the way the van lurched around the corner? He couldn't put his finger on it—but he couldn't follow the van. He was supposed to stay on Ninovich. He took out his phone and called for a patrol car to investigate. He watched the closed doors to the warehouse. How much longer was Ninovich going to be here? His back teeth were floating. Maybe there was enough time to make a quick trip behind the dumpster.

8

THE EXCHANGE

At 8:15 on Monday morning, Detectives Gower and Johnson sat across the desk from O'Brian in his office at the Solomon Island Casino Resort. CSI had finished processing the casino, hotel lobby and restaurant yesterday, but uniformed officers were still searching the island.

"What can I do for you?" O'Brian asked.

"Mr. O'Brian," Detective Gower said, "thanks for meeting us so early. Yesterday we counted four employees missing after the kidnapping. I sent over ten driver's license copies."

"I've got them right here." O'Brian tapped a stack of paper on his desk.

"Did any match?"

O'Brian shifted in his seat. "Could you tell me where you got these photos?"

Gower shook his head. "Police business."

"Two of them are hotel employees. A receptionist and a maintenance technician. They're on top."

Gower looked at the pictures. JB Turner and Lulu Osmond. Two of the five bodies from the van that left the Fifth Street warehouse. He passed them to Johnson.

O'Brian continued. "We haven't been able to get in touch with them."

"You won't be able to. They're in police custody."

"Really? You think they're connected with this crime?"

"All I can say is that they're part of our investigation. Thanks for your help."

Gower and Johnson stood up.

"Detective, I'd like to get our contractor in here working on the repairs. Do you know when you'll be done with the physical investigation?"

"Uniforms should get done searching the island today," Gower said.

"So we can get started tomorrow?"

"For the interior work? You can get started today, but construction workers can only go straight from the ferry into the building."

"Thanks."

Gower and Johnson walked down the hallway, past the rubble in the lobby, and out the front doors. "So two of the bodies were Solomon Island employees," Johnson said. "What do you think? Inside players?"

"Looks that way. And the other three were probably in the robbery crew," Gower said.

"If the bodies in the van are connected with the kidnap/robbery. Could be an entirely separate beef. How much headway have we made with the mope who was driving the van?"

"Charles 'Chucky' Bowmont? He works for Deluxe Paint and Body Shop."

"That's one of Ninovich's shops, isn't it?" Johnson asked.

"Yeah, it is."

"But Ninovich's never been involved in a murder before, not here in the city."

"So far as we know."

. . .

As soon as the detectives left, O'Brian got out his smartphone. "Mr. Smithson? The two we found upstairs in the rooms?"

"I know who you're talking about."

"The cops have them."

"Not a problem. They won't be talking to anyone. Anything else?"

"I sent the package."

"I already knew that."

"If there's anything I can do—" Smithson hung up on him.

O'Brian looked out his office window, but he didn't see the woods or the clouds drifting across the sky. The receptionist and the maintenance tech were dead. Smithson was is a foul mood, and he was going to stay that way until his grandson was safe. He blamed him for the kidnapping, thought his lax management was the root cause. O'Brian turned to the to-do list on his computer. He needed to get the damage repaired and get the casino open ASAP. He needed for Martin to come through with info on Lulu Osmond and JB Turner that would help to find the kidnappers. He had to find some way to add value, to prove his value. He hoped nothing bad had happened to the boy.

MEANWHILE, Koenig found Hernandez sitting in the living room of the Ridgewood safehouse looking at something on his phone. Raymond and the others were still asleep. Koenig blew on his coffee. "Walk with me."

They went out into the backyard. All the houses in sight were quiet, as if everyone were at work or school. A dog in a fenced yard ran up to the nearest corner, but it didn't bark.

"What do you think of today's plan?" Koenig asked.

"It's solid, boss. Assuming the meeting place isn't a trap."

"It won't be. They won't have enough time to do anything except show up. And they won't tell the cops. They'll want to kill us themselves. No, I'm concerned about later."

"What do you mean?"

"After Raymond and Sanchez get away, they might be followed.

Someone might interfere. So I want you at the car drop. They'll make it that far on their own, or we're all running for our lives. Take two guys with you. Stay well back, but watch them. Raymond shouldn't know that you're there. Don't get involved unless they get in a situation they can't handle themselves."

"But you don't want Raymond and Sanchez to know?"

"They can't be lazy, expecting help. They've got to believe they're on their own."

"Okay, I'll get it done. You care which guys I take?"

"Take whoever you like. And Hernandez, you've proven that your management material, so I'm doubling your take."

"Doubling? Thanks, boss."

BY THE TIME Koenig's guy called at 2:00 p.m., Ninovich had checked all his boxes. Two million dollars in old bills sat in two medium duffels in the back of the armored Volvo SUV in Smithson's driveway. Remote control transmitters were hidden in the duffels, turned off so their signals couldn't be detected. The GPS dart rifle was in the front seat passenger's side. Max and Kelly Jo had the GPS tracking information and the transmitter controller.

"The shuttered Bon Jest carpet mill," the voice said.

For the ride to the carpet mill, Smithson and his son, Tim, sat in the back, Mario—a large man with a scar running across his shaved head and tattoos on his fingers—sat behind the wheel, and Ninovich sat with the dart rifle. He called Max with the location as they drove across town. Koenig had chosen a great place for the meet: isolated, so they couldn't have extra men in place, but close by a freeway interchange that branched almost immediately three ways —downtown, suburbs, and interstate north—making escape almost certain.

The Volvo SUV was sitting at the south end of the cracked asphalt lot behind the carpet mill at 3:00 p.m. when a black Ford Explorer with tinted windows came into the north end of the lot, swung around to face the exit, and backed up until it was about thirty feet away. Ninovich got out his phone. "Barlow? They're here. It's a black Explorer."

Two men in tactical gear, ski masks pulled over their faces, got out of the Explorer, their assault rifles at the ready. Mario got out of the Volvo.

"Set the money in the middle. One man," the masked man on the right said.

"Do it," Smithson said.

Mario pulled the duffels from the back of the Volvo and carried them toward the Explorer. When he got about halfway across the distance, the masked man held up his hand. "That's far enough."

Mario set the bags down. "Where's the kid?"

"Unzip the duffels."

He unzipped the duffels. They both contained cash, banded with rubber bands.

"Back away."

Mario looked over his shoulder. Smithson nodded. He backed up to the front bumper of the Volvo, his right hand ready to quick-draw his Glock.

The masked man came up to the duffels, pulled a scanner out of his jacket pocket and scanned the bags for transmitters. No bleeps. He nodded to his partner.

The other man opened the passenger door on the Explorer and brought out Mikey Smithson. He was wearing gym clothes that were too big for him. He was blindfolded with a sleep mask, and his hands were zip-tied together. The liftback of the Explorer opened. As the other man walked Mikey toward the duffel bags, the first man picked up the duffels and hustled them to the back of the Explorer. The second man stood with his hand on Mikey's shoulder until his partner closed the liftback, scrambled back inside the Explorer, and tapped the horn twice. Then the second man patted Mikey on the shoulder, spun on his heels, and ran for the SUV, leaving Mikey standing where he was.

Mario ran to Mikey and pulled off the blindfold. "It's okay, your dad and your grandpa are here."

Tim was running toward them. "Mikey! Mikey!"

Mikey's face lit up. He ran for his dad. Tim scooped him up in his arms and rushed back to the Volvo. Mario pulled his gun and started firing on the Explorer. The back glass shattered. Ninovich ran past Tim and Mikey, the GPS dart rifle in his hands. "Keep firing," he yelled.

The Explorer was slowly gaining speed as it headed for the parking lot exit, Mario's shots punching into the back. Ninovich got down on one knee and fired the dart rifle. A GPS tracking dart stuck to the Explorer's liftback.

"You got it," Mario said.

Ninovich got out his phone. "Barlow? They're tagged."

MAX AND KELLY JO were sitting in a freshly stolen white Camry on the next street over. They were currently dressed like office professionals, but they'd brought extra clothes so that they could blend in wherever they went tailing the kidnappers. "We're on."

Kelly Jo pulled away from the curb. Max looked down at the computer in his lap. The tracking dart was moving on the GPS map. "There it goes. It's two blocks over. Next right, then the second left. We don't want them to get too far ahead."

There was no traffic to speak of in the area around the carpet mill, and Kelly Jo caught all the traffic lights. In a few minutes, they were on the beltway. All the lanes were full, but she was aggressively changing lanes, pushing her way through the gaps. Max looked up from the screen. "You should be able to see them."

She scanned the traffic, following the highway onto the overpass. "There they are, up on the bridge." She flipped on her right turn signal.

"What are you doing?"

"They're going downtown. They're going to switch vehicles. We need to get close enough to turn on the transmitters."

"Be ready to jump back out if it's a fake."

They watched the Explorer fly along as if it wasn't going to take the off-ramp. Then at the last minute, it veered hard, scraped the guardrail, and screeched down onto the downtown surface streets. Kelly Jo had finally gotten into the right lane, but there were several cars in front of her, the lead car sticking to the speed limit. She could get into the middle lane, but she didn't have time or the room to pass the whole line before the exit ramp. The car in front of her tapped its brakes.

"Damn it."

She swung onto the shoulder and stomped on the gas, flying by the line of cars until she came out ahead of the lead car just before the exit ramp. She bounced down the ramp, tapping her brakes as she went. "Where is it?"

"I don't know. They're not showing on the map. Take this first right onto Martin Luther King."

They drove down a block of office towers with a parking ramp entrance at the street level. "Can you see them?"

"Nothing on the map. And the transmitters won't turn on."

"They can't be that far ahead."

"Must be interference. Circle the block," Max said.

She took a right. On the backside of the building, the GPS tracking dart reappeared on the screen. "There's the dart. Go back around and into the parking ramp."

She came back around to Martin Luther King Boulevard and drove down into the public parking. Max got out his pistol and chambered a round. "Nice and slow. We want them to think they're gotten away clean."

They rolled through the parking ramp, studying the vehicles, looking for the Explorer. Finally, at the bottom of the ramp, they found it, broken back window and bullet holes. The men and the duffel bags were gone. Max pulled the GPS dart off the liftback. "We must have just missed them."

"What about the transmitters?"

"They didn't turn on."

"Guess we need to talk to the attendant," Kelly Jo said.

They drove back up to the entrance and parked in a handicapped space. A black man wearing a hoodie and jeans sat in a little office with the surveillance cameras. Max tapped on the glass in the door. The man looked up. "Yes?" he said in an African accent.

"We want to look at the video footage from the last thirty minutes," Max said.

The man shook his head. "I can't do that."

Kelly Jo sat on the edge of the desk. Max dug in his pocket and pulled out a thick wad of cash. "Have you seen the new fifty-dollar bill?" He thumbed through the wad until he found one and then held it out in his hand.

"You two are criminals. You're going to get me in trouble."

Max turned to Kelly Jo. "I think my feeling are hurt." He turned back to the attendant. "But I'll bite. Why do you think we're criminals?"

"It's the same everywhere. No police badge. No detective badge. No call from my boss."

"This is America, my friend. Do you plan on doing this the rest of your life?"

"No."

"Then you need to build up some savings so that you can make a change."

"Fifty dollars is not savings. Fifty dollars is me losing this job and getting a bad reference."

"Fair enough. One-hundred dollars for the look."

The man looked from Max to Kelly Jo.

Kelly Jo smiled. "We haven't threatened you or offered to hurt you. We're trying to give you money. Who's going to know? And who's going to tell? Not us."

The man nodded his head. Max laid a hundred-dollar bill on the desk. "Let's have a look."

The attendant opened the surveillance program on the computer and backed up thirty minutes. The Explore drove into the parking deck. "Follow that vehicle."

The attendant switched from camera to camera following the SUV. It stopped behind a green Subaru wagon. A man got out of the

Explorer and loaded the duffels into the Subaru. The Explorer drove away. "Okay," Max said. "Can we see the plates on the Subaru?"

The attendant switched to the exit camera. The Subaru came up to the exit, both men in the front seats. The license plate numbers were completely visible. Kelly Jo wrote them down.

"That's it," the attendant said.

"Can we see when the Subaru got here?"

The attendant shook his head. Max laid another hundred on the desk.

"It was here overnight. I know that." The attendant went into the previous day's footage, scanning through the feed at high speed, slowing down for anything that resembled a Subaru wagon. He finally spotted it on the entry camera. Kelly Jo compared the license plate numbers. It was a match. "Great," Max said. "Follow it down to where it was parked."

The attendant switched cameras, following the Subaru to its parking spot. A battered Ford Focus pulled up behind it. The driver got out and got into the passenger's side of the Focus. "We need the license plate on that one," Max said.

The attendant switched to the exit camera. Kelly Jo copied down the license number.

"Do you want to make one more hundred?" Max asked.

The attendant nodded.

"The footage that shows us down at the Explorer—you know what I'm talking about?"

He nodded.

"Make us disappear."

"I can't do that. The police will find that out. I won't lose my job for you."

"Had to ask."

Max and Kelly Jo got back in their Camry, Max driving. As they pulled out of the parking deck, Kelly Jo made a phone call. "Hey, Billy."

"Hey, Missus."

"I need names and addresses to go with two license plate numbers."

"Shoot."

She read him the plate numbers off the Subaru and the Ford Focus.

"I'll call you back as soon as I've got something. Might take an hour."

She turned to Max. "We're all set."

THE SUBARU DROVE into a Save-U-Mart parking lot at the outer edge of the downtown and rolled down the outer row of parking spots until it came to a blue Toyota Prius. Raymond and Sanchez got out of the Subaru, opened the liftbacks of the Subaru and the Prius, and transferred the duffels. The driver of the Prius, blond crewcut and a nose that had been broken more than once, climbed into the driver's seat of the Subaru.

"Bruce, burn the Subaru," Raymond said.

"Got you."

"I mean ashes."

"I understand."

Raymond drove the Prius up and down the nearby streets, making sure he and Sanchez weren't being followed, before he drove out of the city and next door into the suburb of Charming Cove. He drove through the gates of a private golf club and residential community, and wound down the parkway to a group of condos, where he opened a garage and drove in. He and Sanchez each carried a duffel bag into the condo.

Koenig got up from the sofa. He gestured toward the dining room table. They set the duffels down. "Any trouble?" Koenig asked.

"Went off without a hitch."

Koenig opened the bags and poked through the bundles of cash. "Did you find the GPS transmitters?"

"Took a while. They weren't turned on yet."

"When did you find them?"

"Before we switched to the Prius."

"Are you paying attention? Do you see why we have to be careful? Smithson isn't going to make any more mistakes."

Raymond smiled. "We've got the money, don't we?"

"Yeah, but we haven't escaped yet."

"So let's disappear."

Koenig shook his head. "We're going to stay right here, wait for the trail to get cold. No one followed you?"

Sanchez shook his head.

"No," Raymond said.

"Then there's no reason to panic. We're all safe right where we are. Get the money counter and run all these bills. We need to know how much we really have and if any of it is counterfeit. And Sanchez, just to be on the safe side, take these duffels across town and dump them somewhere."

"We already found the transmitters," Raymond said.

"But they weren't turned on. So there could be one you missed," Koenig said. "We're getting rid of the bags."

Sanchez dumped the rubber-banded bundles of cash onto the dining room table and left with the empty duffels. Raymond and the two men who'd stayed back with Koenig started running the money through the money counter and rebanding it in bundles of one hundred bills. While they were working, Hernandez came back with his two men.

"Where you been?" Raymond asked.

"Running an errand for the boss," Hernandez replied. He and his men crowded up to the dining room table and looked over the money like dogs eyeing a steak. "Wow. So this is what two million looks like."

The man working the money counter smiled slyly. The other men murmured and nodded like the team that had won the championship.

"Where's the boss?" Hernandez asked.

"In his bedroom," Raymond replied.

Hernandez went down the hall and knocked on the door.

"Yeah?"

He went in. Koenig lay on the bed. He had a magazine in his hand. "How did it go?"

"They lost their tail at the parking deck, stopped in an alley but didn't get out of the car, and then swapped out to the Prius."

Koenig nodded. "What did the tail look like?"

"A man and a woman, good looking; they moved like they knew what they were doing."

"But Raymond lost them at the parking deck?"

"Yes. We never saw them again."

"Keep an eye out for that couple. They are definitely trouble."

MEANWHILE, Detectives Gower and Johnson sat on a sofa in the living room in the Smithson mansion, facing Jeffrey Smithson and his son, Tim. "Let me review what you've told us," Gower said. "You got a call. You went to the old Bon Jest carpet mill. Two employees and your son were with you. There were two masked men in a black Explorer. They had assault rifles. You paid the ransom and got your grandson back."

"Exactly," Smithson said.

"You should have called us," Johnson said.

"Getting my grandson back was the only thing that mattered."

Gower turned to Tim. "Do you have anything to add?"

"It's just like my pop said."

"How much did you pay?" Johnson asked Smithson.

"I'm not getting into that."

"You're not going to tell us what you paid?"

"As far as I'm concerned, this incident is closed."

"There was a kidnapping and attempted robbery. Men died. This case isn't closed until we say it's closed," Johnson replied.

Gower continued. "What are the names of the employees who were with you?"

"David Ninovich and Mario Guzman."

"We're going to need to talk to them and your grandson."

"You can talk to them, but you won't hear anything different."

"And you're not talking to my son," Tim said. "He's been through a lot. Besides, he didn't see anything. He was blindfolded or they were masked the whole time. He was kept in a room with no windows."

"He must have seen something."

"He's just a kid. His mother is never going to agree."

"Look, I understand your concern. Don't you want these guys caught? How about if we get Dr. Wingate to talk with him?" Gower asked.

"Who's he?"

"She's a psychologist who works with us sometimes. She'd be the only one in the room. You or his mom can be with him."

"How would that work?"

"You'd sign a waiver that she could tell us about anything that could help us with the case."

Tim thought for a moment. "Okay. If Myrna agrees, we could do that."

"We'll contact Dr. Wingate. She'll be in touch to set up an appointment."

Gower turned to Smithson. "We're going to find those kidnappers. But we won't tolerate any street justice. You break the law, you'll be arrested."

"Like I said, we got Mikey back. As far as I'm concerned, this incident is over."

A bodyguard escorted the detectives out to the street. They stood on the sidewalk looking back at the house. "Awfully smug, isn't he?" Johnson asked.

"He's got the kid, so the payback can begin in earnest. But I don't think he knows that we stopped the van last night."

"No, but this definitely puts Ninovich in the middle of this."

"Well, we knew it wouldn't be O'Brian. He's strictly money," Gower said.

"We going to waste the time to talk to Ninovich and Mario?"

"Not yet. We need more people on surveillance. If we had been on Ninovich today, we'd have been at the meet."

"Five bodies and a man and a woman that they let go. I'd like to know who they are."

"I've got a feeling that they're going to be around."

They got into their car. "Pulling in Wingate. What made you think of that?" Johnson asked.

"The kid wasn't going to talk to us anyway. Or tell us anything useful. This way, we're not arguing with the parents, and we might find out something."

THE SUN WAS GOING down by the time Max and Kelly Jo pulled to the curb within sight of a duplex in a neighborhood of small, rundown houses. Overflowing trashcans sat at the curbs in front of some of the houses. Others had children's toys scattered across the yards or grass that needed to be mowed. A banged-up Ford Focus sat in the driveway on the near side of the duplex.

"Is that the address?" Max asked.

Kelly scanned the email Billy had sent her. "Yeah. And the license plate matches. That's the car that dropped the Subaru at the parking deck."

"Knock on the door or kick it in?"

"I'll smooth-talk them."

Just then, a man came out the front door, middle-aged, dark hair, a boyish face. He got in the Ford Focus in the driveway. Kelly Jo scrolled down the email to a driver's license picture. "That's Teddy Daniels—the guy who owns the car."

"Do you think anyone else lives in that house?" Max asked.

"Look at him. He's definitely single."

When Daniels backed out onto the street, they followed. He drove six blocks to The Side Pocket, a neighborhood bar at a busy intersection, and pulled into the pot-holed parking lot behind the building. They parked at the outer edge of the lot just as he got out of his car and went into the back door of the bar.

"I'll go in and get him," Kelly Jo said. "But I'm going to put on something a little more casual first." She reached into the back seat for her bag. She changed into black leggings, a long, loose top, and black flats, and untied her hair to let it hang down her back.

"That's a good look," Max said. "I'll get into position."

Kelly Jo strolled into the dimly lit tavern. Two pool tables took up the center of the space, a long bar ran down one wall. There were eight people playing pool. Seven men in jeans and T-shirts and a woman wearing a skirt so short that it was no contest to determine that her preferred underwear was a black thong. Everyone gave Kelly Jo a glance before they turned back to the pool tables, but she had her game on. She was just a mom from the neighborhood. Never been here before. A little lonely, a little needy, not used to drinking. She sat down at a stool one stool away from Daniels. The bartender, black golf shirt stretched over his beer belly and silver hair slicked back from his face, stepped over to her. "What you having?"

"Gosh," she said, "I don't know. A white wine, I guess."

Daniels glanced at her. She smiled. He turned back to his beer.

She peered around nervously. The bartender brought her wine. "Thank you," she said.

Daniels glanced at her again. "Haven't seen you around here before."

"I've never been here before. I don't go out much."

"I'm Teddy."

"I'm Mandy."

He looked at his beer.

Kelly Jo smiled. "Tell me, Teddy, is this place usually this quiet?"

"Friday, Saturday night, happy hour, otherwise it's about like this. That's why I like to come here."

"Not too loud."

"That's right."

"You can carry on a conversation."

"Yep."

"What do you do for a living?"

"I'm a heating and cooling technician."

"You like it?"

"Yeah, yeah, I do." He sipped his beer. "What do you do?"

"I'm in a call center. Part-time."

"Part-time. You a mom?"

"Yes, I am. Two daughters. You?"

"No kids." He pointed at her wedding ring.

"Don't mind that," she said.

MAX WAS WAITING around the corner of the building with a Taser in his hand, standing in the weeds by the air-conditioning compressor, when they came out the back door. He heard Kelly Jo do her drunken giggle. "I hope you don't think I'm too easy," she said.

"No," Daniels replied. "No, I don't. I know how it is. Sometimes a person is just lonely."

Max stepped out from the side of the building. There was no one in the parking lot beside the three of them. He slipped up behind Daniels and zapped him with the Taser. Daniels crumpled to the asphalt. They picked him up by his arms and dragged him to the Camry, where they zip-tied his hands behind his back and loaded him into the trunk.

"Took you a little while," Max said.

"Had to do it right."

He pulled Daniels's keys out of his front pocket. "You take his car."

They drove back to Daniels's duplex. Max pulled up in the driveway. Kelly Jo parked Daniels's Ford Focus on the street. Even though the duplex was dark, Kelly Jo knocked on the door before she used the key to open it. She turned on the light in the living room. It was the usual bachelor untidiness: dirty glasses on the end tables, dust, carpet in need of a good vacuuming. Max was waiting at the trunk of the car. They opened it. Daniels's eyes were open.

"We don't want to hurt you," Max said. "You tell us what we need to know, we'll be on our way."

"My wife gets off work soon."

"There's no woman here," Kelly Jo said.

They helped him out of the trunk and walked him into the house, one on each side of him. Kelly Jo shut the door behind them. "It's just like my partner says. You tell us what we need to know, and we're gone."

Max pointed to the sofa. "Sit."

Daniels sat on the sofa. He glanced from one to the other, back and forth, and then suspicion turned into comprehension. "That fucking Bruce. This is about that car, isn't it?"

"Keep talking," Max said.

"Bruce gave me a hundred bucks to pick him up from the parking garage where he left the Subaru."

"How good of friends are you?"

"I don't have nothing to do with whatever this is. I knew the hundred was too much for what he asked me to do, so I figured the money was for keeping my mouth shut. But I don't owe him anything."

"What's his address?"

"890 Broken Tree Lane, number 214."

"Don't make us come back."

"That's the truth."

Max nodded. "What kind of man is he?"

"What do you mean?"

"Is he a hard guy?"

"Thinks he is. Used to box when he was a kid."

"He run with a crew?"

"I don't know. He does this and that. Works construction."

Max turned to Kelly Jo. "What do you think?"

"Cut him loose."

"Lean up." Max cut the zip tie with his lockback knife. Daniels sprang up from the sofa and stood with his back to the wall.

"Relax," Max said. "We're out of here."

"You did the right thing," Kelly Jo said.

Daniels slammed the door behind them. After they got in the Camry, Kelly Jo got out her phone, opened her map app, and input the Broken Tree Lane address. "Back at the boulevard, take a left," she said.

. . .

MARIO, Sally, and Rita sat in tan minivan down the street from Daniels's duplex. They had been following Max and Kelly Jo all day. Sally was tiny, less than five feet tall in flats, and dressed like a teenage girl, with her blonde hair in bunches at the side of her head. Rita was tall and dark, dressed in black jeans and purple sweater. After they watched the white Camry drive away, Mario pulled into Daniels's driveway without turning on his headlights. Sally hopped out of the van. She knocked on the door. Daniels opened it, a confused look on his face. "Yeah?"

She sprang up, punched him in the throat, and pushed her way into the house. Mario and Rita hurried in behind her. They dragged Daniels up onto the sofa.

"We don't have time to play fuck around," Mario said. "What did you tell the other two?"

"What the hell?"

"The other two. What did you tell them?"

"What is this? A fucking bad movie? Bruce's address. 890 Broken Tree Lane, number 214."

"Who's he?"

"He's the guy who planted the Subaru at the parking garage."

Rita pushed a pistol up under his chin. "Where's the money? Where's the guys who kidnapped the kid?"

"I don't know. I don't know anything."

Mario patted his cheek. "I believe you."

Rita and Sally gripped Daniels's arms. Mario pushed his knee into Daniels's chest and pulled a plastic bag over his head. Daniels kicked and bucked for a few minutes, gasping into the plastic, but they held him down until he stopped moving. Mario checked Daniels's throat for a pulse. Dead. The women let go of him.

Mario rolled up the bag and put it back in his pocket. "Let's get out of here."

MAX AND KELLY JO parked in the visitor parking of the Broken Tree Apartments outside building 892, and walked down the sidewalk to building 890. There was no one on foot, no one in the parking lot, no one driving by. Max had his hands in his jacket pockets, his right hand around the butt of his gun. "What do you think? Missionaries? We haven't done that one in a while. Just in case Daniels didn't know what he was talking about."

"Have you heard the good news?" she replied.

Max picked the lock on the outer door to building 890. They took the stairs up to the second floor. Noise from the apartments seeped into the hall: unintelligible voices, music, TV. The paint was fresh and the carpet was clean. At apartment 214, Kelly Jo knocked on the door. No answer. She knocked again. No answer, no barking. Max picked the lock, pushed the door open and flipped the light switch with the back of his hand. The living room was sparsely furnished. Two chairs and a TV. A kitchen table with four chairs sat near the galley kitchen. Kelly Jo pushed the door shut behind them with her foot. They walked down the hall. The bathroom was empty. In the bedroom, a man was lying on the bed, dressed only in a pair of jeans, the needle still in his arm, a bag of white powder on the night table.

"I'm guessing that's Bruce," Max said.

"Way too convenient," Kelly Jo replied.

"Have you touched anything?"

She shook her head.

"Let's get out of here."

On their way out, Max wiped the front door with a dishtowel. They didn't speak until they were back in their car. "We were lucky no one saw us coming or going," Max said.

"You think it was Koenig tidying up?"

"Most likely."

"What now?"

"We're back to the Subaru. Koenig's guys used it, so it must have been stolen. But where was it stolen, and where was it found?" He started the car. "Give Billy a call. See what he can turn up. We'll start fresh tomorrow."

· · ·

BACK AT THE Charming Cove condo, Koenig was in his room with the ransom money, the other men were watching mixed martial arts on the pay-per-view, and Raymond and Hernandez were back in the far corner of the kitchen, whispering.

"It's a shame we missed our chance today," Raymond said.

"There was no chance. The boss had me following you."

"Then it was a good thing that I don't trust Sanchez. What did you see?"

"You were tailed to the parking deck," Hernandez said.

"Let me guess. A man and a woman, the man forgettable, the woman remarkable."

"That was them."

"The boss pulled them into this job to be part of our patsy team. We left them behind on the island to take the fall," Raymond said. "Smithson was supposed to waste his time interrogating them."

"Then they wriggled out somehow."

"They must be chasing the money."

"Just like the rest of us," Hernandez said. "So when's our next chance?"

"The boss will create a diversion, probably more than one, to execute his final exit strategy. That'll be our next opportunity."

9

TIT FOR TAT

A little before 9:00 a.m., O'Brian stood in the lobby of the Solomon Island Hotel, talking with the general contractor hired to oversee the repairs. The concrete rubble from the explosion had been cleared away and scaffolding with drop cloths hung around the work area. A forklift moved a pallet of concrete blocks to the masons who were repairing the wall.

"How soon?" O'Brian asked.

The contractor pointed toward the damage. "We caught a break. The engineers determined the surrounding structure was solid, so on our expedited schedule, we'll be putting the finishes on the wall next week."

"What about the dust?"

"Every step of the way gets cleaner from here."

"And the electrical?"

"It all tested out as safe."

"So if we post employees to keep guests out of the work area, we could reopen the hotel and restaurant now."

"That's your call. We can stage our materials overnight when traffic is slowest."

"What about the casino floor?"

"Sprinklers did a lot of damage. All the carpets, some of the gaming tables and slot machines need to be replaced. I've got my materials on rush order, and I'm coordinating with your guy—"

"Stewart?"

"Yeah, Stewart. So if we're all cleaned up when the new carpet gets here, you could open part of the casino by the end of next week. The rest of it depends on when your new equipment arrives."

"That's working twenty-four hours a day?"

"I'm afraid so."

"Okay. Thanks for your help."

"You bet."

O'Brian's phone rang. It was Martin, his IT manager. "What's up?"

"I found what you need," he said.

"I'll be right down."

O'Brian took the elevator down to Martin's office. Martin was a skinny kid with a short haircut and an Old Testament beard. Four computer servers sat on shelves on one wall of his office and three huge monitors ran across the top of his desk. He pushed an office chair toward O'Brian when he came through the door. "Have a seat, sir."

"What have you got?"

"The two targets were all over the island, which made it challenging to sift through, but I finally got down to two associations that seem strong. They were both with this couple, Kelly Jo and Max Barlow..." He put a picture of them up on the screen. "Lots of hanging in hallways and loitering that you wouldn't expect, and that's when I found this." He played footage of Cassady, Lulu, and Kelly Jo. They started out in the hallway outside Cassady's office, disappeared into the office, and then reappeared and rushed down the hall to the First Aid office.

"You don't have video inside the rooms?"

"No, sir. But from what we see in the hall, it looks like the sexcapades."

"Anything more?"

"Oh yeah." He started the footage back up. JB crossed the hall from a closet and went into Cassady's office. He came out before Cassady left the First Aid office.

"Has anyone else seen this?"

"No."

"Let's keep it that way. Play the tape again."

Martin rewound the footage and played it again.

"So it's Cassady, Lulu, and—who's the other woman?"

"Kelly Jo Barlow. She's a receptionist."

"And the other guy connected with Lulu and JB is her husband?"

"Max Barlow? Yeah. He's a maintenance tech, just like JB."

"Thanks, Martin. Put a copy of the Cassady footage on a memory stick for me."

O'Brian walked down the hall to the elevator. Cassady. It made so much sense. That's where Turner and Osmond got the room safe master passcode. And the Barlows—the other two employees who were unaccounted for—must have been in on it as well. He pictured Cassady the last time he saw him—stupid grin, ingratiating manner, eyes swiveling around at women's backsides. He had sucker written all over him. It was time to find out exactly what he'd done. O'Brian pressed the elevator button. His luck was finally beginning to turn. He could feel it. Pretty soon he'd have news that Smithson would want to hear. The casino up and running and the traitor found. He'd get out of the dog house and everything could get back to normal.

MIDMORNING, Detectives Gower and Johnson sat in Still Waters Psychology Associates in a side office drinking coffee from paper cups and watching the window to the hallway. Myrna Smithson escorted Mikey out of Dr. Wingate's office, her arm around his shoulder, a tissue balled up in her hand. Gower and Johnson waited for them to turn the corner before they came out into the hall. Dr. Wingate stood outside the door to her office. She was fiftyish. She had a motherly smile and wore a sweater and a loose skirt.

"Hey, Doc," Gower said.

"Hi, Sam, Jamil, come on in."

They stepped into her office: dim lights, loveseat, and two soft chairs. "Anything good?" Gower asked.

"The boy's going to be all right, I think. I'll be seeing him individually and doing a few sessions with the family. But so far as clues..." She shook her head.

"Nothing?"

"The kidnappers made sure he didn't see anything useful. And he'd been taught to cooperate, so he didn't try to find out anything. Very smart."

"It was worth a try," Gower said.

"If anything comes up, I'll let you know."

ACROSS TOWN, Kelly Jo was sitting at the kitchen table in the Tulip Street house drinking coffee and reading the news on her smartphone when Max came into the room with his phone up to his ear.

"Thanks, Billy." He put his phone in his pocket.

"So?"

"Subaru is in the police impound lot. It was stolen from a strip mall on Mission Avenue. Cops found it in the parking lot of Bayside Park. Gas had been poured in it, but for some reason, nobody had thrown the match. Forensics is going to be slow because of the fumes and fire risk."

"Sloppy work," she said.

"It's not Koenig's style."

"You think Raymond came up short hiring Bruce?"

"Might be why Bruce is dead. Any coffee left?"

"You can finish mine." She handed him her cup.

He gulped the lukewarm coffee and set the cup down on the table. "Let's go down to the strip mall and have a look around."

They came off the beltway onto Mission Avenue. Car repair shops, tire stores, sheet metal fabricators, electrical supplies. A few blocks down, they came to a strip mall that bordered a neighborhood of small house and duplexes. Max pulled into the parking lot.

"So this is where the Subaru was reported stolen?" Kelly Jo asked.

"Uh-huh."

"There's a minimarket, a donut shop, a drycleaner, and a liquor store. What would make you think that this was a good place to steal a car?"

"All short-term traffic."

"And I see two surveillance cameras without even looking hard."

"Out in the open for deterrence."

"Exactly."

"This is our guy," Max said. "This is his thinking: We're using the car tomorrow, so by the time it's reported, cops won't be looking for it until after we're done. It'll be sitting nice and safe in the parking garage in the meantime. So there's no reason for me to go all the way across town to pull a vehicle out of long-term parking."

"Bruce, you think?"

"Yeah. Maybe he was a junky. So who dropped him off to steal this car?" He nodded up at the surveillance camera next to the donut shop sign. "I'd like to get a look at that surveillance footage."

"Why? It'll just be another best friend or another stolen car."

"Because Koenig is hiding around here somewhere. That's the way he works. They're hiding, waiting for the heat to die down before they make a run for it. Within a week, everyone's tired of looking, they get lazy, they've got work to do, then it's easy to escape. How far away did these guys go to steal the cars they used? The cars were all taken before the heist. Did any of these guys go all the way across town? Koenig would never make a mistake like that, but he can't supervise everyone. Where did the Explorer come from?"

"I'll call Billy."

An hour later they were eating lunch in Buena Suerte, a mom-and-pop Mexican restaurant. The inside still looked like the Burger King that it had originally been, but the dining room was crowded with construction workers and delivery drivers.

"Great tacos," Kelly Jo said.

"Yeah, this place was a great find." Max pushed his plate away. He'd eaten his burrito and beans, but he'd left the rice.

"You're done?"

"Too much food."

Her phone rang. All she said was "Hey" and "Thanks."

"Billy?"

"Yeah. The Explorer was taken off the street about six blocks from that strip mall."

"Well then. It's time to find out if Koenig found the transmitters in the ransom duffel bags."

TIM AND MYRNA SMITHSON were sitting on a glider on their screened-in porch, holding hands and watching the birds fly to and from the bird feeders set up in the backyard. Mikey was up in his room, playing videogames.

"So we're going to go for a few sessions," she said.

"Mikey going back to school tomorrow?"

"Yes. He seemed perfectly fine. I was the one who was crying."

"It was scary," Tim said. "The worst nightmare scenario. Hard to get adjusted."

"I'm looking over my shoulder."

"I've hired a security team just like we talked about. They'll start tomorrow. Twenty-four seven. I don't think we've got anything to worry about, but it's worth the peace of mind. At least until the police finish investigating."

"I can't help thinking that Mikey is blocking his emotions."

"That's why we're taking him to Wingate. I've checked up on her. Everyone says she's the best."

"What's your dad doing about all this?"

"I don't know. And I don't want to know. That would be getting into his business."

"But you're not the least bit tempted?"

"Would I like to find those assholes and make them suffer for what they did? Yes, I would. God help me, I want it so bad. But you can't stop knowing whatever you find out, and then you have to live with that. Going with Pop to get Mikey is one thing—there was no way I wasn't going to go. But the rest of it—that's not our life. That's not the life we're making for Mikey."

DETECTIVES GOWER and Johnson parked on the street behind Daniels's Ford Focus. The neighbors on the other side of the duplex —a woman and a grade-school boy—were carrying groceries into their house.

"Okay, so Daniels—" Gower started.

"Or Daniels's car," Johnson said.

"—picked up the guy from the parking deck who left the Subaru for the guys who dumped the shot-up Explorer."

"That's what the parking deck surveillance showed," Johnson said. "This is definitely the car. But the house looks empty."

"We'll see," Gower said. "I'll take the back."

Johnson banged on Daniels's front door. The woman next door, bags in her arms, stopped to watch. Johnson held up the badge that was hanging from a chain around his neck. "Have you seen Mr. Daniels, ma'am?"

She shook her head. "Not today. He should still be at work. Is he in some kind of trouble?"

"We just need to talk to him. Is that his car?" He pointed back at the Ford parked on the street.

"Yeah."

"Does he usually drive to work?"

"Always."

The boy was holding their front door open. "Mom," he said.

"Got to go." The woman disappeared into her side of the duplex.

Johnson tried the door. It was unlocked. He pushed it open. Daniels was sitting on the sofa in the dark, his head angled down as if he were asleep. "Mr. Daniels." He didn't move. "Mr. Daniels. Police."

Johnson peered into the room, but he couldn't see anything out of the ordinary. "Mr. Daniels."

He crossed to Daniels and checked his neck for a pulse. He was lizard cold. Johnson flipped the light switch with his elbow and walked through the kitchen to the back door. Gower was on the back steps. "He's dead," Johnson said.

Gower took out his phone and called it in. They stood out in the front yard and waited for CSI. "We're a little too slow," Gower said. "We might have saved his life if we got to him first."

"But we didn't get him involved in this mess," Johnson replied. "He did that all by himself. Look at the bright side. The kidnappers are still around here, cleaning up loose ends."

"You sure about that? Maybe it's Smithson's guys tracking down their money."

"We've got the Subaru. They didn't have a chance to burn it. It's going to tell us something."

"Maybe too late to help."

"Sam, these stumblebums have already made two mistakes. They didn't take the surveillance footage at the parking deck, and they didn't burn the car."

"You're right. They're sloppy. They'll make more mistakes. We've just got to find them faster," Gower said.

"We're going to catch up. We always do."

"You wanted to see me, Mr. O'Brian?" Johnny Cassady stood in the doorway of O'Brian's office. O'Brian sat behind his desk. Joe Brinkley, the hotel general manager, sat in one of the chairs facing him.

"Johnny, I'm glad you could come in on such short notice. Shut the door and have a seat next to Joe."

"Hello Mr. Brinkley," Cassady said. He sat down.

"Let's get right to the point." O'Brian took the memory stick he'd received from Martin, plugged it into his laptop and queued up the hallway video. He pushed the laptop around so that Cassady could see the screen. Brinkley clicked on the arrow to start the video. Cassady watched Lulu and Kelly Jo move him into his office; then a few minutes later, all three of them, locked together, rushed down to the First Aid office.

"I can explain," Cassady said.

"Medical emergency?" O'Brian replied.

Brinkley clicked on the stop button. "The truth is the only thing that can save your job."

Cassady sucked in a breath as if he'd just come up out of the water. "I know I shouldn't have done it. But look at the time stamp. I was off duty. It wasn't sexual harassment. I didn't intimidate them or offer them anything."

"How many times have you done this?" O'Brian asked.

Cassady looked from O'Brian to Brinkley and back. "On the island? This is the only time, I swear. I've met women in town, after work, but not here."

O'Brian looked at Brinkley.

"Sounds about right," Brinkley said.

O'Brian nodded. Brinkley restarted the video. Cassady watched JB go into his office and then come out before he left the First Aid office.

"I don't know anything about that," Cassady said.

"You left your office unlocked," O'Brian said.

"It was a mistake."

"That guy and Lulu Osmond are in police custody."

"They were involved with the robbery?"

"You let your little head tell your big head what to do and look what happened."

Brinkley closed the laptop. "I pulled the personnel files for these employees. JB Turner. Lulu Osmond. Kelly Jo Barlow. And her husband Max. Guess who hired them?"

Cassady looked down at his hands. "I did."

"An amazing coincidence, don't you think?"

"We were shorthanded. They had excellent work records. I called the references."

"How much did they pay you?" Brinkley asked.

O'Brian picked up his desk phone. "Why bother to listen to this liar? I'm calling the police."

"Please don't call the police," Cassady said.

"How much did they pay you?" Brinkley repeated.

"One thousand apiece."

O'Brian hung up the phone. "I hope it was worth it. You're fired. Security will escort you off the island."

"Please, please, please, give me one more chance. I didn't know."

"Exactly." O'Brian buzzed his secretary in the outer office. A uniformed security officer opened the office door. O'Brian looked hard at Cassady. "Get out."

Cassady opened his mouth as if he were going to speak, but said nothing. He slunk out of his chair.

The security officer shut the door behind them.

"What an idiot," O'Brian said.

Brinkley pushed the laptop back toward O'Brian. "As I've already said, sir, I hired him. I take full responsibility. I thought he had potential, that we'd shave off the rough edges, but I was wrong."

"I want a personnel review of all the management and supervisory staff."

"Yes, sir."

"Up until now, your work here has been excellent, Joe. Get these reviews right, and we'll be able to move forward."

"Thank you, sir." Brinkley got up.

"Leave the door open."

O'Brian pulled the memory stick from the laptop and put it in his top desk drawer. He hadn't been hands-on enough. He'd given Brinkley too much latitude. Never again. He was going to get out from under this problem. He was going to eat as much crow as he had to eat to get back into Mr. Smithson's good graces. He was going to save his job and protect his family. He opened his laptop and found Cassady's personnel file—address, phone, email, next of kin—and selected *Print* from the menu. Mr. Smithson would definitely want a copy.

. . .

AT THE CHARMING COVE CONDO, Raymond, Hernandez, and three other men sat at the kitchen table playing rummy. Koenig was in the living room, tapping away on his laptop computer. His phone rang. "Yeah?"

"Mr. Koenig? It's Zeb."

"I know who it is."

"Max and Kelly Jo are still tracking you."

"I know."

"And the cops are following them."

"Do you have an address?"

"Based on his cellphone? Yeah." Zeb gave him the Tulip Street address. He wrote it down.

"Thanks. I won't forget your help."

"You're continued business is all the thanks I need."

Koenig ended the call. He hollered into the kitchen. "Raymond?"

Raymond scooted his chair back from the table and took a sip of coffee before he went into the living room. "What do you need, boss?"

"You took care of the guy who provided the Subaru?"

"Tied off tight. A complete dead end."

"Max and Kelly Jo are still nosing around."

"They won't find anything there."

"But they're still muddying the waters. Smithson should have killed them by now, which means they've squirmed out somehow. Take two guys and deal with them before Smithson or the cops get any closer. Here's the probable address." He handed him a scrap of paper.

"Consider it done."

MAX AND KELLY JO were driving through the neighborhood behind the strip mall on Mission Avenue, Kelly Jo behind the wheel, Max with a laptop open in his lap, clicking the controller to turn on the transmitters that Ninovich had planted in the ransom duffel bags and watching the GPS map to see if they came on. They drove up eight blocks, turned right one block, and drove down eight blocks, going back and forth.

"Nothing," Max said.

"How far away can you remotely turn on the transmitters?"

"Maybe a hundred yards."

"Needle in a haystack."

"If they had been turned on to begin with, Koenig's guys would have found them before they put the money in the Explorer. This was just in case of emergency."

"Well, this is an emergency." Kelly Jo turned right. "This next pass completes the square."

"The neighborhood is changing. Too many homeowners, but not an Airbnb kind of neighborhood. Strangers would stand out. They aren't going to be here."

"Bag it up?"

"Let's go home."

Kelly Jo drove back to Mission Avenue, then down to the beltway, and got off at Fourth Street. In between lunch and rush hour, it was an easy drive, school buses and retirees on afternoon errands. Once she was back on Tulip Street and could see their tiny rental, she pressed the garage door remote control. Just as she began to turn up the driveway, three masked men armed with assault rifles jumped out of a white Suburban parked across the street and opened fire.

"Hurry," Max yelled.

Kelly Jo stomped on the gas and flew up the driveway into the garage. Multiple shots shattered the safety glass in the back window of the Camry. She hit the brakes. The Camry squealed to a stop. She pressed the remote control and scrunched down in the seat. Max was in the floor of the passenger's seat, his arms protecting his head. Bullets punched through the garage door as it lowered to the ground.

Kelly Jo pushed open her door and fast crawled into the kitchen, Max at her heels. Bullets shattered the windows in the living room. Max crawled to the living room sofa and pushed it up against the wall under the windows. Then he rolled up on the sofa and started firing out the window. Kelly Jo crawled up beside him. The three men,

Kevlar vests over their street clothes, were spread out and advancing toward the house. Bullets were pouring in. Kelly Jo and Max fired back as best they could, but they were outgunned. One of the men fell.

"Get our go bag," Max said.

Kelly Jo crawled through to the bedroom, grabbed their go bag from under the bed and started back into the living room when the firing stopped. Max was on his feet. "They ran. God knows why. Let's get out of here."

Sirens screamed in the distance. They hurried into the garage. The Camry was riddled with holes. Kelly Jo tossed the go bag into the back seat and climbed into the driver's seat. Max kneeled in the back seat to knock the broken safety glass out from the edges of the back window so it wouldn't be as obvious that the window was shattered.

Kelly Jo shoved the key into the ignition and gave it a turn. The Camry sputtered to life. "Whew."

Max looked over his shoulder. "Have a little faith."

She pressed the garage door remote. The door screeched up. No one started shooting at them. She sped down the driveway, whipped the wheel, and took off out of the neighborhood. Max climbed from the back to the front seat. "That went a lot better than I thought it would."

Kelly Jo laughed. "I think that's what they call a 'hail of bullets.'"

"We need a new car."

"Let's grab something quick before the cops spot this wreck."

Max point up to the next corner. "Take a right. We'll leave this on the street and pick up something behind that Caffeination coffee shop."

She parked in a no parking zone. "We need to wipe down this car."

"No time to do a decent job. Wipe the wheel and the door handles. Maybe a tow truck will find it before the cops."

They got out, Kelly Jo carrying their go bag, and strolled into the Caffeination parking lot, keeping their backs to the camera mounted on the building. There were five cars in the parking lot, all empty. "Something old," Max said.

"How about that red Chevy?" An old Impala sat in the far corner.

"Looks like an employee car, doesn't it? Won't turn up missing until shift change. Hand me some latex gloves."

She took black latex gloves from the go bag. They put them on while they walked to the Chevy. He picked the door lock and hotwired the car. The back seat was full of fast-food trash and old mail. "Stealing this car is doing this guy a favor," Kelly Jo said.

Max drove around the block to avoid driving by the front of the coffee shop; then he took it easy, driving just under the speed limit all the way downtown and into a parking ramp next to an office building. On the third level, they pulled into a space beside a blue Toyota RAV4.

"This is more our style."

"Cops will find this Chevy when the RAV is reported."

"But they won't be looking for the RAV until tomorrow at least, so we might as well be comfortable while we look for a long-term solution."

Max took twenty dollars from his pocket and dropped it on the floor of the Impala.

"You're getting soft."

"Just hoping to improve our luck."

A few minutes later, they drove out of the parking ramp, making sure to cover their faces when they passed the exit camera. Traffic was beginning to pick up as more and more people got off work. Max took the ramp onto the beltway.

"That was some hard shooting," he said.

"Yeah, but we were punching above our weight. We got one of them and didn't get a scratch," she replied.

"Your range time is paying off."

"I didn't shoot that guy. You didn't shoot him?"

"Not me."

He got into the right lane to take the next off ramp. "I knew

Smithson had a transmitter on us, but he must be actually tailing us. Can't be any other explanation."

"Wants to make sure he gets his money back."

He pulled up to the stop sign at the bottom of the ramp. "Wants to make sure he gets his revenge."

MEANWHILE, Mario was in the minivan tailing the two men in the Suburban as they moved north, circling and backtracking to discover if anyone was following them. He smiled. They wouldn't find him. This was his bread and butter. He'd taught classes on urban surveillance after his fifth tour in the sandbox. Rita and Sally had gotten out of the van when the two guys had run back to the Suburban. They'd no doubt found a ride and were still following Max and Kelly Jo, but this was too good an opportunity to pass up. The Suburban might lead them up the food chain quicker than the grifters, and the sooner they could kill them, the better off they would be. The grifters were the loosest of loose ends, and he didn't want Mr. Smithson, or even Ninovich, for that matter, blaming him if they got away.

The Suburban pulled into a Walmart. The parking lot was half empty. Mario pulled in after it and parked with a good view of the outer lot. He got a pair of binoculars out of the glovebox. The Suburban parked next to a green Jeep Grand Cherokee at the edge of the lot. Two men got out—no Kevlar, no rifles—and climbed into the Jeep. As they started to drive away, another man, an old guy wearing jeans and a ball cap, got into the Suburban. Mario tossed the binoculars in the passenger's seat. This was a well-oiled machine. A man hanging around just to take away the evidence. He followed the Jeep.

The Jeep circled around before getting on Twelfth Street heading north into Charming Cove, where it drove through the gates of Charming Cove Golf Estates. Mario followed along the parkway that ran along the edge of the golf course to a row of condos near the entrance to the clubhouse parking lot. He watched the Jeep park in the garage to condo 793. He pulled over and got out his phone. "Ninovich?"

"Yeah?"

He explained what had happened.

"Great news," Ninovich said. "Sit tight, I'm sending some guys to help you."

Mario glanced up and down the street. He couldn't stay where he was. He was out in the open. But there was a cul-de-sac of two-story houses about half a block away. He drove up into cul-de-sac—five brick houses with ornamental front porches—circled around, and parked facing out where he had a good view of condo 793.

IN THE CONDO, Raymond and Sanchez stood in the living room, explaining to Koenig what had happened. "So you were blindsided?"

"We were caught in a crossfire," Sanchez said.

"We didn't know about the extra guys they had watching their place," Raymond said.

"Are you an idiot? That wasn't them," Koenig said. "There was no coordination of effort, was there?"

"No," Raymond replied.

"That was Smithson's people."

"Smithson's?"

"Yes." Koenig went to the front window and peeked through the closed blinds. "Did anyone follow you?"

"No."

"We're not taking any chances. We're changing houses. Get the bags out of my room."

Koenig and Raymond drove away from the condo in a BMW, Raymond driving. Hernandez, Sanchez, and the other three men waited in the garage in the Jeep. When the BMW passed through the gates to the main road, Koenig called Hernandez. "You can leave now. Tell me what you see."

Raymond turned left, then took the next right, drove four blocks and took another right. Koenig's phone buzzed. "Yes?"

"A tan minivan is following you."

"We'll use the traffic to box them in at the next light." He ended the call.

"We've got a tail?" Raymond asked.

"Tan minivan. Stay in the right lane. Slow down a little bit."

"Catch the stop light?"

"Exactly."

Raymond turned onto Francis Scott Key Drive and slowed down just enough that the other cars were starting to pass him. The traffic was heavy, both lanes full of anxious drivers in a hurry to get home. He glanced in his rearview mirror. There it was. A tan minivan situated behind a red Smart Car and next to a pickup truck.

MARIO WAS three cars behind the BMW. He was sure that the driver had been one of the shooters at Max and Kelly Jo's safe house. When the BMW turned onto Francis Scott Key, he called Ninovich and filled him in.

"Let me know where they land," Ninovich said.

Up ahead, at the intersection, the traffic light turned red. All the cars stopped. Mario glanced in his rearview mirror. Two men wearing ski masks and carrying assault rifles were rushing up on him, one on each side of the minivan. He clawed down into the floorboard for his sawed-off shotgun.

THE MASKED MEN emptied the magazines of their assault rifles into the minivan, shattering the windows and pocking the exterior with holes. Then the man on the driver's side switched magazines, opened the van door, and fired two shots into Mario's head. He looked at the pickup truck to his left. There was no one in the cab.

The traffic light turned green. "Let's go," the other man yelled. They ran back to the Jeep and climbed in the back. Hernandez shoved the Jeep into Drive, jumped the curb, drove the sidewalk to the intersection, and bounced down onto the street.

Up ahead, Koenig and Raymond had turned in their seats to watch. "Now that's how you spring a trap," Koenig said. "Simple, but effective."

DETECTIVES GOWER and Johnson stood in the front yard of the little house on Tulip Street. An outline in the grass marked where the shooter had fallen. Tags indicated the location of shell casings. The CSI team was still on site, men and women in white coveralls carrying equipment in and evidence out of the building. "So the other two missing Casino employees, a man and a woman, were staying here?" Johnson asked.

"Conrad over at Homicide called me. Neighbors identified a man and woman coming in and out over the last few days. Old man across the street—day gambler, rides that bus that goes around town picking up seniors—said she reminded him of a receptionist at the hotel. When they showed him photos of the two women, he made a positive ID. Kelly Jo Barlow."

"But the guy?"

"That's a stretch, but it makes sense; one of the missing guys is her husband, Max Barlow. Three men in body armor came here to kill them. Innocent bystanders don't get that kind of attention," Gower said.

"So whose team are they on? Kidnappers or Smithson? Tell me we got lucky with the fingerprints."

"The dead guy was a career criminal, out-of-towner. No connection with Smithson's crew so far. But there's a lot of fingerprints inside, so it's going to be a while."

"Any blood in the house?"

Gower shook his head. "None thus far."

"So three guys came to kill the Barlows. One got killed. Maybe not Smithson's crew. So how do the Barlows fit into this? They ran off. They've got to hide somewhere. We should get their pictures out to state police and all the motels in the area."

Gower's phone rang. He took the call. "Thanks, Park."

"One of Ninovich's guys got ambushed in his car on Francis Scott Key. They're still working the scene."

"So the war is out in the open," Johnson said. "Guess I'm going to be late for supper."

"You and me both."

MAX AND KELLY JO sat at the little table by the door in their room at the Budget Inn. They'd switched cars again, dumping the RAV4 for a black Honda CR-V they'd taken from the airport long-term parking lot right after a man and woman wearing vacation clothes had dropped it off and rolled four big bags to the passenger pickup shelter.

"Where do you want to go to dinner?" Kelly Jo asked.

"Let's go through a drive-through at some other interchange. We need to keep as low a profile as possible."

She studied his face. "What are you thinking about?"

He smiled. "Koenig set us up perfectly. Got away clean. Left us holding the bag. Put his boys on us without breaking a sweat. Would have got us if Smithson hadn't been tailing us."

"Then why aren't you pissed?"

"Because this puts him at ease, which gives us our first advantage. We're going to mind fuck him, make him believe we're screwed, just a step too slow. Then we are going to pounce, kill him, steal the money, skim off a hundred thousand dollars that we blame on him, and give the rest back to Smithson."

"You're completely insane."

"Yep."

She laughed. "It just might work."

AT JANGO'S SUPPER CLUB, Smithson and Ninovich stood out in the parking lot well away from the valet parking kiosk. Two of Ninovich's crew, in ties and jackets, stood watch at both ends of the lot. Smithson fidgeted with the inhaler in his hand. "So Koenig's guys got away?"

"Yeah, they ambushed Mario on the street just like we were in Juarez or somewhere."

"I saw the picture of the van on the news. Did he have any family?"

"A little old mom in a care center."

"Make sure she's taken care of."

"We'll make sure her bills are paid and her account gets topped off."

"But you've still got the other two? Max and Kelly Jo?"

"They've moved to a motel. Sally and Rita are on them."

"Do we need someone else?"

"Sally and Rita are the best. They won't lose them, and they won't get spotted."

"Why can't we just put a transmitter on the new car?"

"Max and his woman change out cars like underwear. Besides, we may need to help them out of another jam before we're done with them."

Smithson nodded. "They're certainly shaking things up. It was a smart move turning them loose. As long as Koenig wants them dead, they're useful."

"We still came up short. Lost Mario."

"It's a shame about Mario, but that's the closest we've come to Koenig so far. Don't let his people slip away next time." He glanced at a Cadillac that was prowling for a parking space. "O'Brian found the leak."

"Who was it?"

"An assistant manager. Idiot didn't have a clue that he was being used."

"You want him taken care of?"

"Not yet. O'Brian's investigating the hotel and casino management. I want to know the scope of the problem before we do anything." Smithson patted Ninovich's shoulder. "Find Koenig."

Ninovich watched Smithson hobble into the restaurant. That went better than he thought it would. Smithson wasn't blaming him for Mario's death—still saw him as part of the solution, not part of the problem. But the clock was ticking. He needed to find Koenig before Smithson's patience ran out. O'Brian, on the other hand, was screwing himself. The harder he worked to clean up the mess, the more incompetent he made himself look for letting it happen. Good intentions counted for nothing. Only results mattered. So he had to make sure he captured Koenig before O'Brian got his house in order.

10

ONE LAST PLAY

The next morning, before Max and Kelly Jo had left their motel room to go to breakfast, there was a knock at the door. Max peered through the peephole, his pistol in his hand. A police badge blocked his view. "Hey, honey," he called back into the room, "the cops are here."

He slipped his gun into the pocket of his sports coat before he opened the door. Kelly Jo came out of the bathroom buttoning the top button of her shirt. Two plainclothes detectives stood in the doorway, a tall black man wearing a leather jacket and jeans and a blocky white man wearing a charcoal suit.

"Max Barlow?" the black one asked.

"Yes?"

"Can we come in?"

Max stood out of the way.

"I'm Detective Johnson and this is Detective Gower. We'd like to ask you a few questions."

"Do we need a lawyer?"

"Have you done something wrong?"

Kelly Jo leaned against the back of a chair. "What are your questions?"

"Why did you run from the casino?"

"Run from the casino?"

"You work at Solomon Island. You ran after the attempted robbery."

"We were afraid," Max said. "Nobody knew what was going on there. Something blew up in the building. We got out of there as quick as we could."

Johnson turned to Kelly Jo. "Why weren't you at the reception counter?"

"I was on break. We were out in front, so we ran onto the ferry."

"That isn't what the surveillance video shows."

"I don't know anything about that. I just know what we did."

"Then why didn't you come forward afterward?"

"We didn't know anything. We were outside, and then we left."

"Then why did they come to kill you?" Gower asked.

"Who?"

"You've been staying at a rental on Tulip Street since the robbery."

"Until yesterday, when some guys shot the place up," Johnson added.

Max cut in. "You think it was the casino robbers?"

"Who else?" Gower asked.

"Why would they be after us?"

"You tell us."

"I don't know. Maybe they think we're witnesses."

"Maybe. Or maybe you all had a falling out about the money."

"What money? I thought you guys stopped them."

Johnson turned to Kelly Jo. "Did you leave a shot-up Camry behind the Caffeination coffee shop on Randal Street?"

Max and Kelly Jo looked at each other as if they were entirely mystified.

"We're taking prints from Tulip Street and from the Camry," Gower said. "They're going to match. What are we going to find when we run them through the database?"

"I don't know," Max said.

"One of Smithson's crew was murdered up on Francis Scott Key shortly after your place was shot up," Gower said.

"Saw something about it on the news," Kelly Jo replied.

"Somebody's hard after you two." Gower handed Max a business card. "When you decide you've had enough, you give us a call."

"Are we done here?"

"For now."

The detectives left. Kelly Jo peeked through the blinds to watch them get into a blue sedan. "They're gone."

"And we're not arrested, so these identities must still be good," Max said.

"Or they're using us for bait. They didn't have any trouble finding us."

"Which means they're not going to pounce when the fingerprints come back."

"Are you in the new database?"

"I don't know. The system wasn't digital the last time I got busted."

"And that was a long time ago—before we got together. What are the chances that somebody took the time to scan them in?"

"Too many variables. Might have been too smudged to scan. Might not have been scanned. I'm not worried. So who do you think is tracking us? Smithson for sure, probably the cops, and Koenig's crew could show up anytime."

"Definitely."

"We look like completely clueless mopes. It's perfect."

"So what now?"

"Smithson's guy must have tracked Koenig's boys from our house. Which means Koenig's been flushed out of his hidey-hole. He won't take the chance of being found. He's moved to a backup place, a new neighborhood, a place where no one notices people coming and going, few kids, not a motel. He's got too many people with him, and he won't give up his protection just to blend in, not yet, so a by-the-month rental in a marginal neighborhood where people don't trust the cops or help nosy strangers. And they're not suspicious of white guys."

"That's a tall order."

Max got out his phone and clicked on a map app. "He doesn't like the country. Once you're found, you're found." He pulled up a map of the city and started examining the neighborhoods. "Have a look," he said. He sat on the side of the bed. She sat down beside him. "What about over here next to the old warehouse district? Lots of ways in and out."

"That's a big area to cover. What makes you think we're going to have any better luck than when we were hunting the transmitter?" she asked.

"We've got nothing better to do. We'll do a *Where's Waldo* after breakfast. Maybe we'll get lucky."

WHEN THE POLICE detectives arrived at the Budget Inn, Sally and Rita were sitting in a banged-up Toyota Corolla at the far end of the parking lot, sipping on takeout coffee while they watched the door to Max and Kelly Jo's room. "Here comes that pain-in-the-ass Gower. Who's the black guy?" Rita asked.

"The black guy is Jamil Johnson, I think."

"Aren't they the casino robbery cops?"

"They're organized crime," Sally replied.

"We should call Ninovich."

"Let's wait to see if they take them."

When the cops got back in their car, Sally got out her phone. "Ninovich?"

"Yeah?"

"The casino robbery cops were just here at the motel, talking to Max and Kelly Jo."

"Really? How long?"

"A few minutes."

"Thanks for the heads up."

JOHNSON TOOK a right out of the Budget Inn parking lot. "We should have arrested them. You know there were guns in that room. They dumped the Camry, boosted the Chevy from the Caffeination coffee shop, and left it in the parking deck when they took the RAV. We're going to match up their prints. They're professional thieves. They belong in jail."

"I'm all for marking down a win," Gower said. "And we will put them inside before this is over with. But right now, they're trouble magnets. They got away from the island, and we don't know how. They're connected with the kidnapping, and somebody—not Smithson—wants them dead. The earlier bodies could have been either side cleaning up. But Tulip Street and Francis Scott Key are definitely the kidnappers hitting back, which makes the Barlows our best lead to finding the kidnappers and putting an end to all this street killing."

"Okay, I hear you. But if we're going to use them, we've got to have surveillance on them twenty-four seven."

MAX AND KELLY Jo drove down into a neighborhood of small houses that had once been the homes of the union warehouse workers before the commercial docks closed. They saw retirees out on porches, corner boys working their territories, FOR SALE signs in weedy front yards, but no evidence of Koenig or his crew. When they got back the Budget Inn, Ninovich was waiting in front of the door to their room.

"Remember me?" he asked.

"Yeah, you left a definite impression," Max said.

"You going to invite me in?"

"Here's good."

"What did the cops want?"

"What they always want. A free ride."

"Did you like the help you got with Koenig's guys?"

"That was you?"

"We need to help each other."

"How's that?"

"Right now, you're an endangered species. I hold the keys to your cage. But it's your lucky day. I don't care about you. So you're going to give me half of what you're planning to skim from what Koenig stole, and I'm going to let you escape."

"You call that a fair deal?"

"I do."

"But first we've got to find him."

"I've got confidence in you. Either you're going to find him, or he's going to find you. When that happens, you're going to give me a call. I'll let you make your play, and we all get what we want."

"So the two women who've been following us are yours?"

"Yeah, they work for me."

"You play straight with us, we'll play straight with you."

"You keep in touch."

"As soon as we know anything."

They watched him walk back to his Mercedes Benz. "He's going to fuck us the first chance he gets," Kelly Jo said.

"Of course," Max replied. "But now we know who the shadows report to, and we're got a little more room to run."

KOENIG SAT in the living room of a vacation rental house up the coast thirty minutes from Bathsheba City. He had his escape packet—new ID, new passport, new bank account—and the two million. Smithson's people didn't know where he was. Max didn't know where he was. This was exactly the point in the job where his own crew members might decide he'd outlived his usefulness, which meant it was time to create the confusion that would enable him to get away clean. "Raymond."

"Yeah?"

"Have you found Max and Kelly Jo?"

He nodded. "Yeah. They're at a Budget Inn. Two women are watching them."

"Smithson's people, no doubt."

"Clean them all up?"

"Not so fast. We're going to play with them first. Since Smithson doesn't want them dead, we're going to create another diversion. You're going to meet with Max."

"Meet with him?"

"You're not up for it?"

"I'm up for anything."

"That's the spirit. You meet him, tell him we want him off our backs, that we'll give him a hundred fifty thousand to get lost. He'll want to meet me. You say no but finally agree. Both of them must come—Max and Kelly Jo. You make sure the two women see you. You give them enough time to report in before you kill them."

"Why not just kill Max and Kelly Jo as well?"

"We want Smithson to feel betrayed—to be looking for Max, thinking he killed those two women and skipped. We want Max thinking we really are going to pay him off. Then we kill him and Kelly Jo at the meet. Dump them somewhere quiet. Smithson can waste his time searching for a dead man."

"What if he slips out of the trap?"

"Not this time."

"But what if he does?"

"Smithson will still be after him, and we'll still have the money."

At 6:00 P.M., when Raymond pulled into the Chanticleer restaurant, he spotted the beat-up Corolla in the outer row of parking spots. It was well placed to see the front of the restaurant without being obvious. And both of Smithson's women were in the front seats, the tall one and the tiny one. So Max and Kelly Jo had to be inside. Raymond parked up against the far side of the restaurant and strolled around to the front entrance so that the women would be sure to see him. The restaurant was full. Several couples were waiting to be seated. Raymond spotted Max and Kelly Jo seated at a table near the back and wove his way through the other diners to reach them.

"Easy now," he said, sitting down at their table. "We don't want any killing with all these witnesses."

Max kept his hand in his jacket pocket. "What can I do for you?"

"We want to buy you off."

"Finally talking sense."

"We'll give you your one hundred thousand."

"That was before you tried to kill us. I'm touchy that way."

"What's your number?"

Max turned to Kelly Jo. "Honey, why don't you go to the Ladies?" She scooted up from the table. Max continued. "Tell you what we're going to do. You give me a hundred and sixty thousand—that's everything I was promised—and I meet with the old man, we've got a deal."

"No way. You deal with me."

"Then let's find out who Smithson catches up with first."

"You're bluffing."

"I meet Koenig, or we're done."

"Okay, I'll check with him. I can't promise anything, but I'll check."

"I'm sure you'll be convincing."

"But if we meet, it's both of you."

"She's not at the table, is she? I'm dumping her before I get the cash."

Raymond smirked. "So that's the way it is."

"That's the way it is."

"We meet tomorrow. Give me your phone number."

Max wrote on a scrap of paper and pushed it across the table to him.

"I'll call with the time and place." Raymond got up from the table and walked through the swinging doors into the kitchen. It was a cacophony of clattering dishes and shouted orders.

A manager standing in the aisle talking to a server stood in his way. "Sir, you can't be back here."

Raymond pushed past him. "I know. I'm on my way out."

He strode past the short-order cooks working at the stoves and the assistants prepping the plates as if he were in his own kitchen, went by the walk-in freezer and out the back door. He pulled on throw-away latex gloves as he continued around the back of the building and up the sidewalk behind the cars parked in the outside row of the lot. The women were still sitting in the front seats of the Corolla. The tall one was talking on the phone. He squatted behind the car next to theirs and waited until she put her phone away. As he put his hand on the bumper to stand up, a couple carrying a baby came out of the restaurant and started across the parking lot to their car. He crouched back down. When he saw their car turn out onto the street, he glanced both ways, pulled a Sig Sauer from his jacket pocket, stepped up to the Corolla's passenger side window and fired four times.

The first shot shattered the window and went into the tall woman's shoulder. The second shot went into the side of her head, splattering the tiny woman as she reached into her pocket with one hand and grabbed at the door handle with her other hand. The third shot went over her head, but the fourth shot caught her in the neck. Raymond hunched down between the cars. No one was on the street. He scurried behind the parked cars back the way he'd come. Once behind the restaurant, he fast walked back around to where his car was parked and drove away.

KELLY JO STOOD in the hallway to the restrooms and waited for Raymond to leave before she came back to the table. Max had a satisfied look on his face. "What did you work out?"

"They're going to give us the hundred and sixty thousand to get lost. We're meeting with Koenig tomorrow. Time and place to be determined. You're not invited. He thinks I'm dumping you."

"So I'll be working the perimeter?"

"Absolutely."

"Think he'll try to kill you?"

"Of course. But this is our best opportunity to put Ninovich on them, and the two women he's got following us should help even the odds."

Four shots popped off in the parking lot. They both glanced toward the front windows, but they couldn't see anything. A few other customers seemed to know what the sound was, but most seemed oblivious. "That can't be good," Kelly Jo said. "Not in this neighborhood."

Max motioned to their server. "Check, please."

RAYMOND DROVE AROUND for a while to make sure he wasn't being followed before he drove back up the coast to the vacation rental. Koenig looked up from his laptop when Raymond came in the door from the garage. "Did you get it done?"

"Max bought it. Though I had to promise him a hundred and sixty thousand."

"You have to respect his work ethic. He never stops grifting. Are they both coming?"

"He's dumping her before he collects the cash."

"I don't believe it. I told you both of them had to come. We'll need to send someone to take care of her after he leaves for the meet." Koenig frowned. "What about Smithson's shadows?"

"They're dead."

"Good. I've found what looks like the perfect place for the meet. Have a look at the map."

Raymond looked at the laptop screen. Koenig was inside the property search feature of the city assessor's website. On the screen was a map view of a parking lot behind an empty building. It was enclosed by buildings on all sides except for one driveway that ran between two buildings from Jennifer Street.

"A fire burned through this area after an earthquake. Most of the buildings are abandoned. So no witnesses and plenty of time to set up. One way in, no way out. Take Hernandez with you and walk it off. If it's as advertised, we'll send Max there tomorrow."

"Shouldn't one of us stay with you?"

"I'll be fine with the other guys. I need both of you studying the ground."

BACK AT THE RESTAURANT, Detectives Gower and Johnson stood in the parking lot watching the tow truck haul the Corolla away. "What do we know about these women?" Johnson asked.

"The little one I've seen before. She was one of Ninovich's, so I'm guessing fingerprints will tell us the tall one was as well. That makes five bodies in the last two days. Four of them on the street in broad daylight, three of them from Ninovich's crew."

"Crooks killing crooks. It's a win-win."

"For now. But the lieutenant is feeling a lot of pressure to get results. And Max and Kelly Jo were eating here when it happened," Gower replied.

"That's no coincidence."

"Why wasn't our surveillance up on them yet? If we'd had them covered, we would have had an officer right here when it happened."

"You're preaching to the choir. I'll dig into it. We'll have them covered tomorrow."

"We've got to do better. We can't let these mopes slip through our fingers."

MAX AND KELLY JO were sitting up in bed in their motel room watching the late-night news. They saw the film footage of the shot-up Corolla being pulled by the tow truck. "That must have been Raymond," Kelly Jo said. "He got up from the table and went straight for them."

"If we didn't have a deal with Smithson, he might have thought we did it," Max replied.

"Tomorrow is the endgame."

"Yeah. Koenig will try to kill us."

"But we're ready for him," Kelly Jo said.

"Got aces up both sleeves. Best case scenario: Koenig hands us the one-hundred-sixty grand and Ninovich kills him while we're getting away."

"And the worst case is we're ambushed, Ninovich arrives too late, and we're fighting for our lives."

"How about some positivity?"

"I'll believe we've screwed him when we've screwed him."

11

RUNNING AND GUNNING

At 10:00 a.m., Max got a phone call from Raymond. "There's a parking lot behind an empty storefront on Jennifer Street —used to be a Jumbo Records and CDs. Be there at four p.m."

"Your boss going to be there?"

"He'll be there." Raymond ended the call.

Max turned to Kelly Jo. "We're on for four p.m."

"Let's get ready," she said.

They drove out of the motel parking lot and circled around the block. "Anyone following us?"

"Not yet."

"Google up the storage place."

They drove out to Security First Storage at the northern freeway interchange and drove up and down the aisles until they found the storage unit Anders had set up for them. Max picked the lock and rolled up the garage door. Four large duffels lay on the concrete floor. "Anders came through," Kelly Jo said.

"I wasn't worried he'd put them there. I was worried that he told Ninovich."

They loaded the duffels into the back of the Honda. Then they drove downtown. They cruised up and down until they found a public parking ramp without an attendant. Across the street was Tony's Pizza and Subs. They got a table by the window, shared a pepperoni pizza and a salad, and waited for the noon traffic to die down. Then Max crossed the street and walked the parking ramp until he found an old Ford Explorer. He picked the lock, hotwired it, and tapped the horn once as he exited the lot. Kelly Jo followed him in the Honda.

MEANWHILE, up the coast at the vacation rental, Raymond, Hernandez, and their four remaining men were loading their vehicles. After they dealt with Max and Kelly Jo, there would be no time to waste. They were coming back here, getting paid off, and going their separate ways. Koenig was in the den in the walkout basement. He was taking no chances with his crew members. The two duffel bags of money were sitting on the sofa facing the big-screen TV. Koenig had transferred the entire two million into the right bag and placed one million counterfeit in the left bag. Then he rigged each bag with C-4 on a mercury switch detonator. A quart mason jar of ball bearings was duct-taped to the explosive. If anyone tried to move the bags, they would explode, killing everyone in the room and destroying the money. Unless they input the correct passcode on the remote control.

Koenig slipped the remote control under the seat cushion of the chair next to the sofa. He didn't need to carry it. He just needed it conveniently at hand when he came back, preferably with fewer crew members. He went up the stairs to the main floor. Everyone was sitting in the living room. "Are we ready?"

"All set," Raymond said.

"I've got a good feeling about this," Koenig said. "I can't wait to see the look on Max's face." He turned to Hernandez. "Who's going after Kelly Jo?"

"Cortez," Hernandez replied. "He's already left."

"He knows where to meet us afterward?"

"He'll be there."

. . .

Back at the Budget Inn, Max and Kelly Jo carried the duffels into their room. Kelly Jo took a sniper rifle out of one duffel, assembled it and checked the action. All good. Then she disassembled it back into the duffel and made sure both magazines were full. Meanwhile, Max pulled the assault rifles from their duffels, checked them over, and checked their magazines. Finally, they tried on their comms headsets and earpieces. Everything worked perfectly.

They packed their clothes and shower kits into their roller bags and loaded then into the Explorer. "Looks like we've got a new shadow," Kelly Jo said.

Max nodded. "The red Taurus? So obvious. Must be courtesy of Gower and Johnson. Did you see the other one?"

"The Latino in the old white Saturn?"

"Uh-huh."

Kelly Jo shook her head. "They're going to be tripping over each other."

"That's exactly what we want."

Kelly Jo carried the duffels containing the sniper rifle, her comms, and one of the assault rifles out to the Explorer, while Max carried his comms and the other assault rifle out to the Honda. Then they wiped down the motel room for prints, starting with the bathroom and then working methodically from the back of the room to the door. By 2:30 they were ready.

"See you on the other side," Max said. They hugged and kissed.

"I'll be watching you." Kelly Jo drove away.

Max got in the Honda, unzipped the duffel containing the assault rifle so he'd be able to pull it out if he needed it, and waited. The Taurus was still there, but the Saturn was gone. He called Kelly Jo. "The Saturn is missing."

"I think he's on me," she said.

"Be sure."

"I will."

He ended that call and then called Ninovich. "I'm about to bag up your trash."

"I heard you met with one of his guys yesterday."

"Raymond. Sorry about your women. I think he got them."

"Where are you going?"

Max gave him the address. "Meeting in about an hour. If you hurry, you'll be there in time to clean up the scene."

KELLY JO CIRCLED AROUND A BLOCK, sped through a traffic light as it turned from yellow to red, cut down an alley, and turned right onto a boulevard. No Saturn. She kept on this route until she had to cut over two blocks to stay on course. That's when she noticed the Saturn again. She called Max. "The Saturn? Thought I lost him, but he's back. Seems like he knows where I'm going."

"What street are you on?"

"Orion."

"I'll box him in."

Max looked in his rearview mirror. The Taurus was two cars back, driving like he took the surveillance course, taking it easy, not jumping around attracting attention. Max didn't have time to play it safe. The traffic light ahead was green. He stepped on the gas to gain some distance from the Nissan immediately behind him, then he hit the brakes, skidding for four or five feet. The Nissan braked hard. The Ford behind it did the same, and veered left to avoid a collision. Max stomped on the gas just before the Nissan slammed into him. Both lanes were blocked. The Taurus was trapped. Max shot through the intersection on the yellow light and took the next right.

He drove just above the speed limit, passing cars wherever he could. Three blocks down Orion Drive, he spotted Kelly Jo and the Saturn. He got out his phone. "I'm behind him. We're not going to fool around. Find an alley."

She took the second right down an alley behind a row of small shops. After she saw the Saturn and Max behind her, she stopped just beyond a dumpster and stepped out behind it with a pistol in her hand. A small man wearing dark clothes came out of the Saturn with a machine pistol. Max snatched up his assault rifle and rolled out of the Honda onto the pavement. "Cop?" he yelled.

The small man swung his pistol toward Max. Max fired twice. The man crumpled beside the Saturn. Kelly Jo stood lookout while Max went through his pockets. No money, no wallet, just a pay-as-you-go cell phone. "This is one of Koenig's guys."

There was one number in the address book. Max send a text message: *It's done.* Then he put the phone in his pocket.

"We're running out of time," Kelly Jo said.

"It's not going to start without us. You call me when you're in place."

MEANWHILE, Sergeant Park had driven around the cars blocking Crenshaw Boulevard. He'd seen Barlow's Honda CR-V take the right turn one block past the intersection. He followed. The Honda was nowhere in sight. Park sped up, glancing down the side streets as he shot by them. Just a simple surveillance job, and he'd botched it. Gower was going to ream him a new one. But there was nothing he could do about it now. He was going to have to report in. That's when he heard the gunshots. They were close. He slowed down and started driving up and down the cross streets. A few minutes later, he spotted a man lying in an alley beside the open car door of a white Saturn. There was no one else in sight. He pulled up beside the Saturn and rushed over to the man. No pulse. His clothes were bloody, and a machine pistol lay on the pavement beside him. Park called for police response. Then he called Gower.

"So Barlow made you and lost you?"

"Yes, sir."

"And within eight blocks, you heard gunfire and found a dead man in an alley off of Orion Drive?"

"Yes, sir."

"Near Jackson Street?"

"Yeah."

"Stay at the crime scene. We're coming to you."

GOWER AND JOHNSON were driving down Mission Avenue, Johnson behind the wheel, when Sergeant Park called. "Head for Orion Drive," Gower said.

Johnson took a left at the next intersection. Gower pulled up a city map on a tablet computer. "Orion and Jackson. That whole area is a warren of abandoned buildings."

"That fire was pretty bad in there. Not much left. You think Barlow killed that guy?"

"I think Barlow's up to something and it got that guy killed, so it must be happening now."

"It'll take a lot of manpower to search that area." Johnson took a right onto Crenshaw Boulevard.

"But there's not much legitimate reason for groups of people to be gathered there. And there's been a killing. I'm radioing for the helicopter to sweep the area."

KELLY JO PARKED behind an abandoned three-story building one street behind the shuttered Jumbo Records and CDs. The street was deserted. She slung her assault rifle over her shoulder, put her comms headset into her jacket pocket, and grabbed the bag containing the sniper rifle out of the back of the Explorer. The windows on the building were boarded up, but the padlock on the exterior door had been forced open. The scratches on the metal were new. She gave the door a gentle push. The first-floor landing was dark. She pulled a penlight from her jacket pocket. The stairs were littered with fast-food trash and liquor bottles, but all the trash looked old, like it had accumulated before the padlock. She focused her light on the steps. A large boot print marked the dust. She crept up the steps, straining to hear any sounds as she went. The second floor seemed undisturbed, likewise the third floor. But the dust on the steep stairs to the roof showed definite smudges. She sneaked up the stairs and slowly lifted the hatch. A man with a sniper rifle was lying in position on the roof overlooking the parking lot behind the Jumbo Records and CD. She crept back down to the third floor and called Max. "There's a guy in my spot," she whispered. "Don't want to spook Koenig by shooting him now. Put on your earpiece and microphone. When you tell me you're in place, I'll deal with him."

"Got you."

Max PULLED over on Jennifer Street a block away from the shuttered Jumbo Records and CDs. He called Ninovich. "I'm at the meet. My girl's on the roof."

Ninovich chuckled. "We'll try not to kill you in the crossfire."

Max put in his comms earpiece and clipped the microphone inside his shirt. "Check. Check. Love you."

"Love you more," Kelly Jo replied.

He turned up the driveway between the buildings and into the parking lot. A Toyota Highlander sat across the parking lot, facing him. He had to admire Koenig's choice of a meeting spot; it was the perfect place for an ambush. Only one way in and out. Deep shadow hid the doorways to the building behind the Highlander. He flashed his headlights. "We're on," he said into his microphone. He could hear the chop-chop-chop of helicopter blades in the distance. He wondered if that was Koenig's ride out of here.

He stepped out behind the Honda's door, the assault rifle in his hands. Raymond got out of the driver's side of the Highlander, and then Koenig got out of the passenger's side. "Well, my boy, you certainly know how to be a pain in the ass."

"Thanks," Max said. "But I'm not here to trade pleasantries. Have you got my money?"

Koenig nodded to Raymond, who opened the liftback and came back with a duffel bag, which he tossed toward Max. It landed with a thud about ten feet short of the Honda. Max squinted into the shadows behind the Highlander, but he couldn't see any movement. He kept his rifle trained on Koenig as he stepped around the SUV's door and crossed to the duffel. Money or old newspapers? Joy or murder. He squatted down and unzipped the bag. Rubber-banded bundles of old money.

Koenig watched him with his hands in his pockets. "Hard to believe you would leave your woman."

"Why's that?" Max shoved his hand into the bag to see if it was all money.

"Scuttlebutt says you're soft on her."

"Can't believe everything you hear," Max said. The sound of a gunshot reverberated off the surrounding buildings. He heard Kelly Jo in his ear. "Got him. I'm in place." He zipped the duffel and hoisted it onto his left shoulder.

Koenig kept talking as if he hadn't heard the shot. "No woman and no job. There's nothing for you here but trouble. You might as well come with us. It'll be like the old days."

"I'm out of here," Max said.

As he turned, three men rushed out of the shadows, pistols drawn. Max ran for the cover of the Honda as the men opened fire. Just then a police helicopter swooped down over them, swinging a spotlight across the parking lot. Max, squinting in the blowing dust, fired blind. One of the shooters fell to the ground. He heard Kelly Jo's voice in his ear. "One down."

The loudspeaker on the helicopter crackled. "Put your weapons down. You're under arrest."

Koenig and Raymond ran back toward the Highlander. Ninovich and four men wearing garage coveralls poured down the driveway into the parking lot, firing as they came. Raymond and Koenig's other two men returned fire. Koenig climbed into the Highlander and sped straight into Ninovich's men, scattering them as he escaped down the driveway. Max ran from behind the Honda to the nearest block of apartments, trying doors as he scurried along. A shooter was chasing him. He didn't know if he was one of Koenig's or one of Ninovich's. He turned, fired a burst, and kicked in the next door he came to. He glanced back. The shooter was down. "You got him," Kelly Jo said.

"Get down off there. I'm heading west."

. . .

NINOVICH RAN out onto the street in front of the Jumbo Records and CDs, climbed into his Suburban and started after Koenig, who was about a block ahead of him. He heard sirens. In his rearview mirror he saw the police converging on the parking lot. He'd caught a break. He'd gotten out of there just in time. But if he screwed things up now, Smithson would probably kill him himself. He had to get the money back, and he had to get Koenig. He was slowly gaining on the Highlander as it meandered through the nearby streets. It seemed as if Koenig was trying to determine if he was being followed before he made his next move. Ninovich smiled. He wasn't some greenhorn who would fall for such a simple stunt. In the next few minutes, Koenig would have to telegraph where he was actually going. At Crenshaw Boulevard, the Highlander took a left. Coast Road. He had to be headed for the Coast Road. That was the only artery out of the city in that direction. Ninovich got out his phone. Who was closest?

He called his garage at Sea Side Place. "Freddy? I need a loaded semitruck up at the intersection with the Coast Road, and I need it now."

"It'll be there in five minutes."

"Call me when it's there."

WHEN KOENIG LEFT in the Highlander, Raymond and Hernandez fell back toward the apartment to their right, laying down cover fire for each other as they moved. Both of their men were down and shooters —they assumed they must be part of Smithson's crew—were slowly advancing on them.

"Where's the car?" Raymond yelled.

"On the street behind us," Hernandez replied.

An unmarked police car, blue light pulsing and sirens wailing, screeched to a stop in the driveway to the parking lot. Two cops in plain clothes crouched behind their open car doors, weapons drawn.

"Put your weapons down," the helicopter loudspeakers said.

Raymond and Hernandez ran through the apartment, through the fire damage and abandoned furniture, and out onto the next street over, where a pickup truck sat parked on the street. Hernandez pressed the unlock button on the key fob as they rushed toward it.

"Think we can beat Koenig back to the money?" Raymond asked.

"We're going to try."

MAX COULD STILL HEAR SHOOTING and the chop-chop of the helicopter blades in the distance. He was three blocks from the parking lot, creeping along the side of a row of burned-out houses, the duffel over his shoulder and his rifle down along his leg. He saw headlights flash in his peripheral vision. He glanced over his shoulder. It was the Ford Explorer. Kelly Jo waved from the driver's seat. She pulled up on the street beside him. He tossed the duffel and the rifle into the back and climbed into the front. "How did it end back there?"

She grinned. "Clusterfuck. The cops, Koenig's guys, Smithson's guys, everybody shooting everybody."

"That was some good work back there."

She shrugged. "How did we do?"

"I don't know. I didn't have time to count."

"I'm surprised there was money in the bag."

"I guess he thought I'd shoot him right then if the bag was empty. He was going to take it back after he sprung his trap anyway."

She put the Explorer in Drive. "Koenig got away."

"We'll see about that. Let's go get our escape packet."

KOENIG FELT PRETTY good about his prospects. Most all his guys were dead, and he'd had to leave Raymond behind, but he still had all of the two million. One stop at the vacation rental for the money and his escape packet, and he would be gone, never to be seen again. A citizen of a small Caribbean nation with no extradition treaties. Two more blocks of warehouses, and he'd be on the open road. Two hands on the steering wheel, watch the speed limit, every mile getting him farther into the clear. Sea Side Place was on his right.

When he reached the intersection, a semitruck flew through the stop sign and slammed into his right side. Everything was happening in slow motion. The airbag exploded in his face. The front of the Highlander crashed into a tree. He unhooked his seatbelt, kicked the door open, and fell out of the Highlander into the grass, coughing as he scrambled to his feet. He could hear gunfire. He looked over his shoulder and saw two men climbing out of the semitruck. He ran for the beach, gunshots peppering around him.

NINOVICH SCREECHED to a halt behind the wrecked Highlander and jumped out of the Suburban with his pistol drawn. The Highlander was wedged between a huge oak and the semitruck, its front end crushed. He glanced up at the cab of the semitruck. Freddy, the leader of his Seaside Place crew, and Derrick, one of Freddy's car thieves, were climbing out, their pistols in their hands. "Where is he?"

Freddy pointed with his gun hand. "He ran toward the beach."

"Get after him!"

Freddy and Derrick jumped down from the cab and rushed around on either side of the Highlander. Ninovich opened the back of the SUV. It was empty. He hurried after his men. Freddy and Derrick were on the rocky beach, searching among the boulders and sandy cuts with their pistols out. "Did you see him?"

They shook their heads.

"Any blood?"

"Nothing," Freddy replied.

"Keep looking. He was only a hundred yards ahead."

"It's all gravel here, Ninovich. And the tide is coming in."

"I don't care."

KOENIG WAS IN THE OCEAN, underwater swimming down the beach past the wreck. As long as they did what made sense and kept looking in the other direction, he had a chance. He lifted his head out of the water and glanced back toward them. They were farther away. A craggy boulder jutted out into the surf just ahead of him. Once he got to the other side of it, they wouldn't be able to see him. He spat out water, gulped a breath, and drove under. He'd certainly made a fool of himself getting into a pissing contest with the kid. Hadn't thought he'd be sharing info with Smithson. Should have had Raymond kill him at the restaurant.

He found a handhold on the rough surface of the boulder, lifted his head above the water, and took another breath. He glanced back. No one was coming. He clung to the side of the boulder, moving hand over hand until he was on the far side. Then he climbed out onto the gravel, dripping like a half-drowned rat. He was completely hidden from Smithson's men. A couple hundred yards down the shore, a man and a woman stood at the water, and a dog rushed back and forth, chasing the waves. He felt in his pockets. His lock picks were still there. He strolled over to the on-street parking, approached an old Ford as if it were his, and picked the door lock. Once inside, he hotwired it. Quarter tank of gas. More than enough. The back seat was a jumbled mess of clothes and food wrappers. He found a towel and draped it over his head like a hood before he pulled out into traffic and headed for the vacation rental. The money was waiting.

MEANWHILE, in the parking lot behind Jumbo Records and CDs, Gower and Johnson were directing the cleanup. The police helicopter was gone. Four men were in custody. Two were dead on the pavement, another on the roof of the three-story building to the south. The crime scene investigators had just arrived, but the overall situation seemed clear. Some sort of meeting had gone bad. The Barlows had probably been here, but they were gone now.

"Who are these guys?" Gower asked.

"Two of the guys we arrested definitely work for Ninovich," Johnson said. "The three dead ones I've never seen before. They've got no identification."

"Like the guy in the alley."

"Maybe they belonged to the kidnappers."

"Maybe. We need more facts."

Sergeant Park crossed over to them. "Just got a call. A semi from one of Ninovich's garages T-boned a Highlander up on Coast Road."

"Anyone injured?"

"There's no one there."

KELLY JO WAS PARKED in front of the Bright Smiles dental practice next to the Mail-N-More on Vine Street, downtown. All the stores, except for the Mail-N-More and the corner bar, were closed. She saw a patrol car drive by in her rearview mirror, but it didn't slow down. Max came out of the Mail-N-More with a manila envelope in his hand.

"It's all here," he said. "IDs, passports, credit cards."

Kelly Jo backed into the street. "Are you calling this a win?"

"Yes, I am."

"Koenig could say the same thing."

"I'm not done with him yet. Aces up both sleeves, remember?"

Max called Zeb. "Hey, brother."

"What can I do you for?"

"I reached out to you for info on Koenig, and then Koenig was all over us."

"I didn't have anything to do with that."

"I don't believe in coincidence. I've done a lot of trade with you over the years, but I guess Koenig's done more."

"It's not like that."

"I believe it is. If you want a pass, you're going to have to help me now."

"You can't get to me."

"Can't get to you? Are you on the space shuttle? 'Cause if you're on this planet, you are definitely getable. You want to put a contract on me and find out who's better at running and gunning?"

"What do you need?"

"Where's Koenig?"

The line was quiet.

"Where is he? There's not going to be any blowback, because he's going to be dead."

"Up on Coast Road north of you. Vacation rental place. Let me get the address."

"You do that."

Kelly Jo pulled into a Gas-N-Go and stopped next to the side of the building. "I told you he was a rat bastard."

"Yeah, you did. I thought he just had a problem with women."

Zeb gave him the address.

"This better be right."

"It is."

"We'll see." Max ended the call.

Kelly Jo watched a silver Nissan pull away from the gas pumps before she put the Explorer in Drive. "So, we going after Koenig?"

"No. I've had enough of this mess. We're getting out of town while the getting's good."

"Then what was that about?"

"Listen."

Max put his smartphone on speaker and called Ninovich. "Hey, buddy, how's it going?"

"Fuck you."

"So you haven't found Koenig?"

"I'm going to find you. I'm going to put my hardest guys on you and the little bitch."

"You're hurting my feelings. Didn't I tell you I'd take care of you? Koenig's running up to his last safe house." He gave him the address. "You hurry, you might catch him and the money." Max ended the call.

"You think Koenig is really still there?" Kelly Jo asked.

"Don't know. Maybe we'll get lucky, and they'll kill each other."

RAYMOND AND HERNANDEZ were already at the vacation rental. No one had come after them, so they'd made an easy drive up the coast.

They knew where the duffels were, knew they were wired to explode, and they'd had time to find the remote control. But they didn't know the passcode.

They were in the living room, beers in their hands, assault rifles in easy reach, watching the Coast Road. "How much of that mess do you think was intentional?" Hernandez asked.

"If by intentional," Raymond replied, "you mean planned out in detail, I don't know. But if you mean the general result, the whole mess was intentional."

"Did he get himself killed?"

"He'll be along shortly. He's got the cops and Smithson's crew all over each other and there's only the two of us left, so he'll be crowing when he gets here."

"If he shows, we make it a three-way split, or we kill him after he disarms the bombs."

"He'll want to pay you your twenty-five thousand and for me to leave with him."

"That's a nonstarter."

"Just kidding. A three-way split is fine with me."

"If he doesn't show, we'll have to find a guy who can figure out the pass code," Hernandez continued.

"He'll show."

When the Ford pulled into the driveway, they picked up their rifles and took position where they could each watch the sidewalk and each other. Koenig hurried up the walkway, moving like a crab, his wet suit hanging awkwardly against his body. He turned the doorknob and gave the door a push, letting it slowly open so he could look inside before he entered. He saw Raymond and Hernandez angled off to his right and left. "Boys. Glad you made it."

Hernandez chuckled. "You've looked better."

"I've been better. But it's nothing a drink of whiskey and two million dollars won't fix." He walked past them into the kitchen and poured himself two fingers of scotch. "You find the remote?"

"Yes, we did," Raymond replied.

"Then let's talk about how we do the next little part."

"What do you mean?"

"I think all three of us want to leave here alive. We've earned it. So how are we going to make that happen?"

NINOVICH, Freddy, and Derrick were barreling up the Coast Road in the Suburban. Freddy was pushing the truck like he was on an empty stretch of the Autobahn. Derrick was in the back seat filling the magazine of an AR-15 rifle. Ninovich was on the phone, calling in reinforcements. "ASAP. Don't wait for stragglers. You get in the truck now."

KOENIG, Hernandez, and Raymond were sitting in the living room facing each other, Raymond and Hernandez with rifles across their laps, Koenig holding his scotch. "The problem, as I see it," Koenig said, "is that after I disarm the bombs, we could all turn on each other. No matter what anyone says now, no matter what they promise, the temptation of two million dollars is just too great."

"So what do you suggest?" Hernandez asked.

"We could throw all the guns into the ocean, but then we'd be vulnerable to anyone else who shows up."

"Who else could show up? We're the only ones who know about this place."

"If you believe that, my boy, you're dreaming. Time is of the essence. It always is."

"Then you better disarm the bombs."

"Possibly being killed later is always preferable to definitely being killed now."

"We could unload the guns and put them in our cars."

"Then we just take the bloodbath out into the yard."

Raymond slapped his hand against his thigh. "Two bags, two bombs."

Koenig smiled. "I was waiting for you to figure it out."

"What the fuck are you talking about?" Hernandez asked.

"Is that your best offer?" Raymond asked.

"Absolutely," Koenig said.

Raymond spoke to Hernandez. "He'll disarm one bag. We can take it and leave. He'll stay with the other bag until we're gone."

"If you try to take the last bag," Koenig said, "I'll input the explode code and blow it up. We can all die or you can settle for half a million apiece."

"Jesus," Hernandez said. "You'd kill yourself? And blow up a million dollars?"

"If I'm going to die, everyone dies and no one gets the money," Koenig replied. "What's your answer?"

"You've got a deal," Raymond said.

"I'm in," Hernandez said.

"Okay," Koenig said. "Leave the rifles up here."

They went down into the walkout basement. "The remote is on the mantle," Raymond said.

Koenig got the remote, turned so that Raymond and Hernandez couldn't see what he was doing, and input the disarm code for the left duffel. Then he put the remote control in his pocket. "All done."

"Pick it up," Hernandez said.

Koenig shrugged. He unzipped the left duffel, took out the bomb and the jar of ball bearings, set them on the sofa, and passed the duffel to Raymond. "That should make things lighter."

Hernandez grabbed at the opening to the duffel. It was full of rubber-banded bundles of old one hundred-dollar bills. His eyes lit up. He turned to Raymond. "Let's go upstairs and make a count."

Koenig followed them up the stairs. Hernandez dumped the bundles of bills onto the dining room table. "Fifty-fifty split and go our separate ways."

Raymond counted out two piles of fifty bundles each. Then he and Hernandez thumbed through the bundles in their own pile at random, to make sure the bundles were all money.

"Satisfied?" Koenig asked.

"No," Hernandez said. "I'd like a third of the whole score, but it will have to do."

Raymond and Hernandez bagged up their money. On the way to the door, Raymond turned to Koenig. "See you around, old man."

"If you actually believe you're going to see me again, then I didn't teach you well enough."

Koenig watched Raymond and Hernandez drive away before he picked up the assault rifle from the sofa and went into the bedroom to get his escape packet. It was just where he left it under the mattress. He was all set. He wondered how far they would get before they figured out that the money he'd given them was counterfeit.

He heard a vehicle outside. They couldn't know about the money yet. Did they change their minds about killing him? He rushed to the living room window and peered out through the blinds. Ninovich and two men were climbing out of a Suburban. How did they find out he was here? A Ford F-150 slid into the yard behind them. Christ. Koenig fired a burst through the window. The glass exploded into the yard. Ninovich and his men dove for cover. Three men jumped out of the F-150, firing as they ran for the side of the house. They were going to outflank him. He had seconds, not minutes. He ran down the stairs into the walkout basement. No time to disarm the duffel and escape. The money or his life. Damn it. How did they get here so fast? The kid had done this to him. Had to be him.

Koenig slipped out the patio door into the backyard and scurried behind a garden shed in the back corner just before one of Ninovich's men appeared around the side of the house. The man crept along the house until he came to the patio door. Koenig took the remote control from his pocket. As soon as the man saw the duffel, the money was gone. Either he'd blow it up or they'd call in someone to defuse it. Two million. All gone. It was just a diversion now. Two million for his life. Koenig input the explode code into the remote control.

Two explosions, one on top of the other, rocked the house. Pieces of roofing and scraps of lumber exploded into the sky. Koenig, shielding his head with his arm, rushed across the backyard and into the neighbor's yard. No one appeared to be home. No one who could hear, anyway. He cut through their yard to the next house, where he looked through the glass in the back door of the two-car garage. An old Bronco sat on one side of the garage; the other side was empty. He broke out the glass with his elbow and entered. The back door to the house was open. A key rack hung on the wall just inside the door. Koenig took the keys to the Bronco. This was not a time for stealth. Ninovich and his men were probably dead, but he couldn't take the chance. He raised the garage door and backed out onto the Coast Road. Bits of shingle, broken glass, and splinters of wood littered the yard. A fire truck wailed in the distance. Koenig sped away. All that work, all that effort. For nothing. All the up-front expenses, and purchasing the counterfeit. He'd had to use every penny he could scrape together. The job itself had been perfect. He'd had the two million in his hands. But now it was all gone. He hoped the kid was dead.

NINOVICH STOOD in the front yard of the vacation rental, a bloody gash on his face. His ears were ringing. The place looked like it had suffered a direct hit from a tornado. The house was gone. The yard and street were strewn with lumber, glass, shingles, drywall, and bits of one hundred-dollar bills. What the hell had caused the house to blow up? The guys from the F-150 had died during the blast. A toilet had smashed the hood of the Suburban. The windshield on the Ford truck was shattered.

He felt a hand on his shoulder. Freddy pointed at the truck. He was saying something, but Ninovich couldn't quite make it out over the ringing. Derrick pulled the truck forward. Ninovich nodded. He and Freddy climbed in. They drove down to the nearest side street, where they turned off the main road and pulled over. Ninovich got out his phone and texted for help.

"Little Jimmy will be here in twenty minutes."

Freddy shook his head. "Can't hear a fucking thing."

He showed him the text message.

Little Jimmy, a fat man wearing olive garage coveralls, pulled up in a utility van and transported Ninovich, Freddy, and Derrick to Mendoza and Warren Medical Clinic. A nurse wearing scrubs was holding the back door open for them when they arrived. Before Ninovich got out of the van, he put his hand on Little Jimmy's arm. "Can the Suburban or the Ford be traced back to us?"

Little Jimmy shook his head *no*.

In the clinic, they each went into different treatment rooms. Ninovich sat on the end of an exam table. The nurse took his vital signs. He thought she told him his blood pressure was surprising good considering the situation, but the ringing in his ears was still a little loud for him to be sure. Before she left, the doctor came in and checked him over. Then he picked up a tablet computer, wrote a note, and handed the tablet to Ninovich. *You probably have brain trauma from the explosion. Your hearing will probably improve over the next few days. You should rest for a few days. Avoid loud noises. If your symptoms don't improve, you should seek more treatment. I'll be back to stitch up your face.*

The doctor and nurse left the room. A text message came in on the tablet. It was Smithson. *What?*

Ninovich replied: *Target and $ blown up. Still looking for others.*

You okay?

Except for hearing.

Keep me posted.

There was a knock on the treatment room door. Ninovich deleted the text message from the tablet. The doctor and nurse came back in and directed Ninovich to lie down.

SMITHSON DELETED the text message from his phone. Two million blown up. Who would blow up two million dollars? Crazy, crazy guys. Nobody could have expected that. At least Koenig was dead. Ninovich had gotten that right. And they were still after the others. Before they were done, the world was going to know that they couldn't come after his family.

He walked across the patio behind his house and looked down the riprap to the rocky beach. But what to do about O'Brian? He was a major disappointment. Didn't have control of his people. Didn't know what was going on right under his nose. He was fine for handling the money. Good at schmoozing up the county officials. But that was only half the job. He needed to be reminded of what was expected of him. Smithson speed-dialed him.

"O'Brian?"

"Yes, sir?"

"Have you completed the personnel evaluations of your management staff?"

"Everyone's clean."

"Except the assistant manager."

"Yes, sir."

"Time to tie up loose ends. I want you to take care of him."

"I'll put somebody on it."

"You're not listening. You take care of him. Personally. You do it tomorrow."

"Yes, sir."

HERNANDEZ WAS in the airport bar and grill, nursing a rum and Coke, when he saw the news footage of the rubble at the vacation rental. The wrecked Suburban in the yard must have arrived shortly after he and Raymond left. It appeared he'd made the right decision. He'd put the $500,000 in his checked bag with his shower bag and clothes, dropped his pistol in the airport trash, bought a ticket to Denver. His plane was on time. He was safely within the airport's security envelope.

He glanced at his watch. Time to go to the gate. He finished his drink, ambled down the hallway and turned into the men's room. There was no line. When he came out, two men pulling carry-on bags were behind him, talking about a presentation they had to give. As he continued down the hall, an AUTHORIZED PERSONNEL ONLY door opened ahead of him. The two men dropped their bags, grabbed him by his arms, and rushed him through the door.

The door slammed shut. Two men wearing airport security uniforms were in front of him. He broke free from the men holding his arms, dropped into a boxing stance and stepped toward the men in front of him, swinging at the man on his left. The man shifted out of the way, and the man on his right hit him in the face with a .38. His nose broke, someone hit him from behind, and he fell.

Hernandez woke up tied to a chair next to a mountain of crushed cans in a materials-sorting building at a resource recovery plant. He had two black eyes, and his nose was swollen shut. A bald man sat in another chair facing him, cotton in his ears and a bandage on his cheek. Two big men stood on either side of him. "You're Ninovich."

Ninovich nodded. "See how this goes? You can't save yourself. It's too late for that. You can die quick or you can die slow. And there's no one here to make any judgments about your bravery, so why stretch it out?"

"What do you want to know?"

"Where's the other guy?"

"Raymond? I don't know. We split the million and went our separate ways."

"What did you do with your half?"

"It's in my luggage."

"No," Ninovich said. "The money in your luggage is counterfeit."

"Not possible. I got that straight from Koenig. Your guys are fooling you."

"Maybe Raymond screwed you."

"The money never left my sight. The money was in two bags. Koenig disabled the bomb in one bag, gave us the money, used the bomb in the other bag as leverage so we couldn't kill him and take it."

"Two bags?" Ninovich shook his head.

Hernandez's face fell. "That cheating bastard."

"You idiot. I almost feel sorry for you. Almost."

MAX AND KELLY JO were in a Holiday Inn Express at a freeway interchange. They'd bagged up the clothes they'd been wearing that day, showered, left the clothes in a dumpster, eaten take-out Chinese, and were now sitting on the bed in their underwear watching the late news, the duffel of money at their feet. "That house really blew up," Max said.

"You think Ninovich was in there?"

"I bet he was at the scene. Was he inside? We can only hope."

"Cops haven't released a casualty list."

"They'll have to find enough pieces first."

"Why did Koenig do it? What was his plan?" Kelly Jo asked.

"If he wasn't inside? Something must have gone wrong. Fire can cover a lot of sins." Max kicked at the duffel. "But why did he give us the full one hundred sixty grand?"

"That's what I'm saying."

"All in old hundreds."

"Because they look perfectly good. Serial numbers seem to be different. Paper feels right," she said.

"There's lots of good paper out there. You can order it from China. Not the government paper, but close enough."

"We need a blacklight or a UV light to see if the security thread glows pink."

"Strip club, blacklight bowling, reptile heat lamp," Max said.

"There's nothing open around here. We'll have to figure it out tomorrow."

12

LOOSE ENDS

Friday morning, O'Brian was parked on the street when Cassady came out of a Caffeination coffee shop with a to-go cup. He'd been following him as he meandered around town, stopping at hotels and condo offices as if he was job hunting. Was he really going to kill this kid? It had been so long since he'd killed anyone, or even ordered anyone killed. He kept seeing Cassady's family at his funeral. But it was him or Cassady. Cassady was already a dead man. If he didn't kill him, Smithson would just have Ninovich send someone. And after Cassady was gone, he'd be next. There'd been too many mistakes. That's why Smithson had ordered him to do it, to remind him of his place in the pecking order. If he screwed this up, Ninovich would be coming to kill him. And Ninovich wouldn't flinch.

This time, Cassady didn't get back in his car. He walked down the street and turned into the Saint Denise Cemetery. O'Brian locked his car and took off after him. Inside the gate, the cemetery was row upon row of granite and marble headstones, figures of angels, gigantic family crests from the last century. O'Brian stayed in the shadow of the mature maples that ran around the perimeter, moving as quickly and silently as he could, hoping to spot Cassady before

Cassady spotted him. And there he was, sitting on a bench, his coffee cup on the seat beside him, his attention on his smartphone screen. O'Brian got his hand around the butt of the Glock in his suitcoat pocket as he crept toward Cassady.

Just as he reached the back of the bench, Cassady stood up. He jerked his hand up to his chest. "Mr. O'Brian. You startled me. What are you doing here?"

O'Brian smiled. "I've been looking for you."

"Really? What for?"

O'Brian glance around. There was no one in sight. "I keep thinking about our last conversation."

"Mr. O'Brian. I was such an idiot." He looked down at his feet and rubbed his forehead. "I know you'd never rehire me. But I can't get a job with that bad recommendation...is there any way?"

O'Brian took a deep breath. This was a terrible place to kill Cassady. He'd have to leave the body here. It would be found within hours. But it was the best chance he would get. "Sure," he said.

Cassady looked up. O'Brian pulled the Glock and shot him twice in the chest. The gunfire was louder than he remembered it being. As Cassady crumpled, O'Brian spun around 360 degrees to make sure no one was there. Then he shot Cassady in the head, shoved the gun back in his suitcoat pocket and jogged out of the cemetery.

THAT AFTERNOON at Galaxy Yacht Sales, Smithson, Ninovich, and O'Brian were gathered in Smithson's office. "I'm glad you took care of that problem," Smithson said. "I really am."

"It was my responsibility," O'Brian said.

Smithson turned to Ninovich. "Your guys clean it up?"

"Yeah, dumped him off a boat out in the channel."

"You were following me?" O'Brian asked.

"Two guys," Ninovich said.

"You can see our problem," Smithson said. "You'd made some terrible mistakes. I needed to know I could count on you, but I couldn't chance being wrong. So I had Ninovich put some eyes on it.

Protected us both. Proved you were really with us and got rid of the evidence."

O'Brian looked at Ninovich. "I guess I need to thank you."

"You're great at what you do," Smithson continued, "but you're not boss material. You showed that, too. Ninovich's going to run things."

"Yes, sir."

Ninovich offered his hand. "Nothing will change. You'll take your usual percentage."

O'Brian shook hands.

"I assume you're getting your house in order?" Ninovich continued.

"As we speak."

"Great."

"Change of subject," Smithson said. He turned to Ninovich. "Four of your guys were arrested."

"Not a problem. They didn't shoot at the cops. And it turns out they didn't kill the three dead guys."

"That's some horrible shooting."

"Lucky for us this time."

"So there's no problem?"

"Nothing significant."

"Then we're done here."

Out in the parking lot, Ninovich watched O'Brian drive away. They didn't have Koenig's body, but he had to be dead. That was a hard crash. He must have been disoriented, probably had a concussion, that's how he ended up blowing himself up. Made a careless error. Not that it mattered how it happened. The only important thing was that Koenig wasn't coming back, and Smithson was satisfied. There was only one guy left. Raymond. They were going to find him and make him suffer. Max and Kelly Jo had done their part. He wouldn't have found the house up the coast without them. Not in time. If they stayed away, he'd let bygones be bygones. He climbed into his Mercedes Benz. Of course, he still had to keep an eye on O'Brian. Either he would fall in line, or he would have to go. Only time would tell.

. . .

THE NEXT DAY, Raymond got out of his Jeep and walked up onto the porch of the mountain cabin he'd leased six months ago. He had groceries, internet, and an unobstructed view of the county road winding up the valley. He was going to lay low for a while. Half a million in counterfeit hundreds. He couldn't say that he was surprised. Koenig had kept them all too busy to see everything he was doing. Still, it was better than nothing. He'd need to sell it somewhere. Ten cents on the dollar would net him $50,000, but he should probably keep $10,000 in counterfeit just to make his real money stretch farther. Then, in six months or so, he'd need to set up a scam.

He sat down in the glider on the porch. He's seen the explosion on TV, but he didn't believe for a minute that Koenig was dead. He was out there somewhere. If he had the two million, he probably really was retired. And if he didn't have it, he was building up enough working cash for a new score, and planning how he was going to get even with everyone who'd screwed him out of the two million. Either way, Raymond was going to make sure he was never found. Not by Koenig, or Smithson, or Max and Kelly Jo.

GOWER AND JOHNSON stood in the front yard of the vacation rental up on the Coast Road. This crime wasn't in their jurisdiction—it belonged to the Sheriff's department—but since the fingerprints on a right hand found in the backyard matched a known member of Smithson's crew, they came up to have a look. Lawn scattered with scraps of wood, shingle, and drywall, remaining walls teetering into the open hole of the basement level, a wrecked Suburban in the driveway. It was surprising there was any evidence to be had at the scene—explosion, fire, water damage from putting out the fire—but the Sheriff's department was accumulating a fat file that they were happy to share. They still weren't sure how many had died here— weren't sure they would ever know. They did know that at least one person had left the scene, because a car was stolen from a neighboring house. It hadn't been found yet.

Gower kicked at a piece of brick. "This looks like the endgame of a messy job."

"We can only hope," Johnson replied.

"The butcher's bill has been pretty steep."

"We don't have to clear the ones killed by private security on the island. And Chucky Bowmont is going to eat the five bodies in the van that he drove out of the warehouse if he won't cut a deal."

"That still leaves us Daniels," Gower replied.

"The car guy suffocated in his house? Yeah, that's a tough one. Could be either Smithson or the kidnappers," Johnson said.

"And Bruce."

"The OD? I'm calling that a misadventure."

"What about the others? We've got Mario and the two women from Chanticleer restaurant, plus the guy in the alley and the three behind the record store," Gower said.

"Ninovich's guys aren't talking. Maybe we'll get lucky when the prints come back from the national database, and we'll be able to roll up a few more guys. We don't have near enough to get Smithson or Ninovich."

"And what about the kidnapper? Or the Barlows? We ought to be able to put the guy in the alley on them."

"We have to find them first." Johnson looked at his watch. "It's only eleven-thirty, but I didn't get any breakfast. There's nothing more for us here. You want to go back to town for some early lunch?"

"Sure. How about Cassie's? They have that turkey and gravy special."

"Their coffee tastes burned."

"We'll pull through a Caffeination afterward."

MEANWHILE, Koenig was in the white tablecloth dining room of a cruise ship. His name was Neil Madison. He was a retired money manager. A jovial, well-mannered man who still managed money for close friends. Seated at the table with him were Mr. and Mrs. Talbot, two whitehaired lovebirds who'd found each other after their first spouses had passed away. "You are so fortunate," he said. "I've never found anyone after Annabelle passed."

They beamed.

"How do your children feel about it?"

"It took them a little time to come around," Mr. Talbot said. "But they got there."

Mrs. Talbot smiled.

"Then you're doubly blessed."

"How so?" Mrs. Talbot asked.

"All of your children must be financially secure," Koenig continued. "That's the source of most bickering. Someone counting on an inheritance."

Mr. Talbot put his hand on Mrs. Talbot's. "We are blessed. Completely and entirely blessed."

Koenig smiled to himself. They seemed just a little demented. He wondered how far he could work his way into their lives over the next two weeks. "Well, it was great meeting you. I'm sure I'll be seeing you around."

"We'll be at the ornithology talk this afternoon."

"Really? So will I."

He walked away from the table. A cruise ship was a great place to start over. Lots of suckers and no police. He crossed the lobby to the elevator. He'd have a stake for a new scam in no time.

MAX AND KELLY JO were on the freeway headed south, driving a Cadillac Escalade they'd bought at Wild Bill's Pre-Owned Autos in Sharpsville. Wild Bill had been very happy to take their dirty old money. They'd burned the Explorer in a farm field.

"Koenig," Kelly Jo said. "What a devious bastard. One hundred sixty thousand in counterfeit."

"Like I said, the snake in the Garden of Eden."

"There are easier ways to make a dollar."

"There are. But the satisfaction of screwing Koenig over is mighty sweet. Couldn't have done it without you."

"But we're not going to get to go on vacation."

"Sorry about that. We'll use the counterfeit to set up a new job."

"You really think Koenig is dead?"

"I don't know. But I'm willing to bet he didn't get to keep the two million."

"How do you know?"

"He wouldn't have blown up the house if he had a choice. Not his style. Too much attention. Ninovich must have caught him off guard."

"You think he was really trying to put together his retirement money?"

"Two million would make a nice package, particularly if you screwed all your partners."

"Hard to do by yourself."

"Yes, indeed. Doesn't mean he wouldn't try."

Kelly Jo spotted a state police car parked on the right of way on the opposite side of the freeway. "Trooper with a speed gun pointed at us."

"I see him. I'm not going too fast. Call Billy. See if he has any leads on a potential job."

A NOTE FROM THE AUTHOR

Thanks for reading *The Casino Switcheroo*. If you enjoyed it, please post a review on a review site of your choice. A few words will do. Honest reviews are the number one way I attract new readers. Thanks so much.

I'd love to hear from you. You can reach me at my website: https://michaelpking.org

The Travelers
The Double Cross: A Travelers Prequel
The Traveling Man: Book One
The Computer Heist: Book Two
The Blackmail Photos: Book Three
The Freeport Robbery: Book Four
The Kidnap Victim: Book Five
The Murder Run: Book Six
The Casino Switcheroo: Book Seven